PINOCCHIO

© Copyright View Productions Pty Ltd
First published 1987.

Published by
View Productions Pty Ltd
GPO Box 1858
Sydney NSW 2001 Australia

Printed by
Western Colour Print Pty Ltd
102 Victoria Road
Marrickville NSW 2204 Australia

Collodi, Carlo. 1826-1890.
   (Avventure di Pinocchio. English). Pinocchio.

   ISBN 0 86441 015 8.

   I. Voican, Daniela. II. Title. III. Title : Avventure
di Pinocchio. English.

853'.8

PINOCCHIO

Carlo Collodi

Illustrations by Daniela Voican

View Productions – Sydney, Australia

Contents

HOW IT HAPPENED THAT MASTER CHERRY, CARPENTER, FOUND A PIECE OF WOOD THAT CRIED AND LAUGHED LIKE A CHILD

Once upon a time there was a piece of wood. It was not an expensive piece, just a common block of firewood — one of those thick, solid logs that are put on the fire in winter to make cold rooms cozy and warm.

I do not know how this really happened, but one fine day this piece of wood found itself in the shop of an old carpenter. His real name was Master Antonio, but everyone called him Master Cherry, for the tip of his nose was so round, red and shiny that it looked like a ripe cherry.

When he saw that piece of wood, Master Cherry was very pleased. Rubbing his hands together happily, he mumbled to himself: "This has arrived just in time, I shall use it to make the leg of a table." He grasped the hatchet quickly to peel off the bark and shape the wood, but as he was about to give it the first blow, he stood still with arm uplifted, for he had heard a very small voice say in a beseeching tone: "Please be careful! Do not hit me so hard!" Master Cherry looked so surprised, his funny face became still funnier!

He turned frightened eyes about the room to find out where the little voice had come from and saw no one! He looked under the bench — no one! He peeped inside the cupboard — no one! He searched among the shavings — no one! He opened the door to look up and down the street — still no one! He laughed and scratched his wig. "I can not really have heard that little voice, I must have imagined it!" And he struck a hard blow upon the piece of wood.

"Oh, oh! You hurt!" cried the same far-away little voice. Master Cherry was dumbfounded, his eyes popping out of his head, his mouth gaping wide, with his tongue lolling out. When he regained his senses, trembling and stuttering with fright, he said: "Where did that voice come from, when there is no one around? Might it be that this piece of wood has learned to weep and cry like a child? I can hardly believe it. Here it is — a piece of common firewood, good only to burn in the stove, the same as any other. Yet — might someone be hidden in it? If so, the worse for him — I'll fix him!"

With these words, he grabbed the log with both hands and started to knock it about unmercifully. He threw it to the floor, against the walls of the room, and even up to the ceiling. He listened for the tiny voice to moan and cry, but heard nothing. He tried bravely to laugh — "There can be no doubt, I have just imagined that tiny voice!"

The poor fellow was very frightened, so he tried to sing a happy song to gain some courage. He put down the hatchet and picked up the plane to make the wood smooth and even, but as he drew it to and fro, he heard the same tiny voice. This time it giggled as it spoke. "Stop it! Oh, stop! Ha, ha, ha! You're tickling my stomach."

This time poor Master Cherry fell down in a faint. When he opened his eyes, he found himself sitting on the floor. His face had changed — fright had turned the tip of his nose from red to deepest purple.

MASTER CHERRY GIVES THE PIECE
OF WOOD TO HIS FRIEND GEPPETTO
WHO TAKES IT HOME TO MAKE
HIMSELF A WONDERFUL PUPPET.

That very moment a loud knock sounded on the door. "Come in," said the carpenter, not having the strength left to stand up. At the words, the door opened and a dapper little old man came in. His name was Geppetto, but to the boys of the neighbourhood he was called Polendina, because the wig he always wore was the the colour of a pudding of yellow Indian Corn, or maize, which many poor people ate in those days. Geppetto had a very bad temper which he lost when anyone called him Polendina! He simply went wild and no one could do anything with him.

"Good day, Master Antonio" he said, "what are you doing on the floor?"
"I am teaching the ants their A B C's."
"Good luck to you than."
"What brought you here, friend Geppetto?"
"My legs. And it may interest you to know that I have had a useful idea and have come to ask you a favour, as I wish to start work immediately."
"Well, here I am, at your service" answered the carpenter, raising himself to his knees. "Let me hear your idea."
"I thought of making myself a beautiful wooden Puppet, one that will be able to dance, fence and turn somersaults. With this Puppet I could go around the world, and earn my living. What do you think of that?"

"Bravo. Polendina!" cried the same tiny voice which had so upset Master Cherry. On hearing himself called Polendina, Master Geppetto turned the colour of a red pepper and facing the carpenter, said to him angrily:
"Why do you insult me?"
"Who is insulting you?"
"You called me Polendina."
"I did not."
"I suppose you think I did! I know it was you."
"No!"
"Yes!"
"No!"
"Yes!"
And growing angrier each moment, they went from words to blows, and finally began to scratch and bite and slap each other.

When the fight was over, Master Antonio had Geppetto's yellow wig in his hands and Geppetto found the carpenter's curly wig in his mouth.

"Give me back my wig," shouted Antonio.
"You return mine, and we'll be friends."

The two old men, each with his own wig back on his own head, shook hands and swore to be good friends for the rest of their lives.
"Well then, Master Geppetto, said the carpenter, to show he bore him no ill will, "what is it you need?"
"I want a piece of wood to make the Puppet. Will you give it to me?"
"Gladly," said Master Antonio and went immediately to his bench to get the piece of wood which had frightened him so much. But as he was about to give it to his friend, it jerked violently, slipped out of his hands and hit against poor Geppetto's thin legs.

"Ah! Is this the gentle way, Master Antonio, in which you make your gifts? You have made me almost lame!"
"I swear to you I did not do it!"
"It was I, of course!"
"It's the fault of this piece of wood."
"You're right; but remember you were the one to throw it at my legs."
"I did not throw it!"
"Liar!"
"Geppetto, do not insult me or I shall call you Polendina."
"Idiot!"
"Polendina!"
"Donkey!"
"Polendina!"
"Ugly monkey!"
"Polendina!"

On hearing himself called Polendina for the third time, Geppetto lost his head with rage and threw himself upon the carpenter. Then and there they gave each other a sound thrashing.

After the fight, Master Antonio had two scratches on his nose and Geppetto two buttons missing from his coat. Thus having settled their accounts, they shook hands and swore once again to be good friends. Then Geppetto took the piece of wood, thanked Master Antonio and limped away toward home.

WHEN HE GETS HOME, GEPPETTO MAKES THE PUPPET AND CALLS IT PINOCCHIO.

THE FIRST PRANKS OF THE PUPPET

Little as Geppetto's house was, it was neat and comfortable. It had a small room on the ground floor, with a tiny window under the stairway. The furniture could not have been much simpler: a very old chair, a rickety old bed, and a tumble-down table. A fireplace full of burning logs was painted on the wall opposite the door. Over the fire there was painted a pot full of something which kept boiling happily away and sending up clouds of what looked like real steam.

As soon as he reached home, Geppetto took his tools and began to cut and shape the wood into a Puppet.

"What shall I call him?" he said to himself. "I think I'll call him Pinocchio. This name will make his fortune. I knew a whole family of Pinocchi once — Pinocchio the father, Pinocchia the mother, and Pinocchi the children — and they were all lucky. The richest of them was a beggar."

After choosing the name for his Puppet Geppetto set seriously to work to make the hair, forehead and eyes. Imagine his surprise when he noticed that these eyes moved and then stared fixedly at him. He said in an aggrieved tone: "Foolish wooden eyes, why do you stare at me?" There was no answer. After the eyes Geppetto made the nose, which began to stretch as soon as finished. It grew longer and longer till it seemed endless.

Poor Geppetto kept cutting and cutting it, but the more he cut the longer grew that impertinent nose. In despair he let it alone. Next he made the mouth. No sooner was it finished than it began to laugh and poke fun at him. "Stop laughing!" said Geppetto angrily, but the laughter continued. "Stop laughing, I say" he roared in a voice of thunder.

The mouth stopped laughing, but it stuck out a long tongue. Not wishing to start an argument, Geppetto pretended he saw nothing and went on with his work. After the mouth he made the chin, then the neck, shoulders, stomach, arms and hands. As he was about to put the last touches on the finger tips, Geppetto felt his wig being pulled off. He glanced up and what did he see? — his yellow wig in the Puppet's hand. . . . .

"Pinocchio, give me my wig!" But instead of giving it back, Pinocchio put it on his own head, which was far too small for it. At that unexpected trick, Geppetto became very worried. "Pinocchio, you wicked boy!" he cried out. "You are not yet finished, and you are already rude to your poor old Father. Very bad, my son. The old man felt very sad.

The legs and feet still had to be made. As soon as they were done, Geppetto felt a sharp kick on the tip of his nose. "I suppose I deserve this!" he said to himself, "I should have thought of it before I made him. Now it's too late!" He took hold of the Puppet under the arms to put him on the floor to teach him to walk. Pinocchio's legs were so stiff that he could not move them, and Geppetto held his hand and showed him how to put out one foot before the other. When the legs were limbered up, Pinocchio started walking by himself and dashed all around the room. He came to the open door, and with one leap he was out into the street. Away he ran!

Poor Geppetto ran after him but was unable to catch him, for Pinocchio ran in leaps and bounds, his two wooden feet, as they beat on the stones of the street making a lot of noise. "Catch him! Catch him!" Geppetto kept shouting, but the people in the street, seeing a wooden Puppet running like the wind, stood still to stare and laugh at his antics.

At last a policeman came along, who, hearing all the noise thought that it might be a runaway horse and stood bravely in the middle of the street, firmly resolved to stop it and prevent any trouble. Pinocchio saw the officer from afar and did his best to escape between the legs of the big fellow, but without success. The policeman grabbed him by the nose (it was an extremely long one) and returned him to Master Geppetto.

The little old man wanted to pull Pinocchio's ears. Think how he felt when, upon searching for them, he discovered that he had forgotten to make them! All he could do was to seize Pinocchio by the back of the neck and take him home. As he was doing so, he shook him two or three times and said to him angrily. "We're going home now. When we get home, then we'll settle this matter!"

Pinocchio, on hearing this, threw himself on the ground and refused to take another step. One person after another gathered around the two. Some said one thing, some another. "Poor Puppet" called out one man. "I am not surprised he doesn't want to go home. Geppetto, no doubt will beat him unmercifully, he is so mean and cruel!"

"Geppetto looks like a good man," added another, "but with boys he's a real tyrant. If we leave that poor Puppet in his hands he may tear him to pieces!" They said so much that, finally, the policeman ended matters by setting Pinocchio at liberty and dragging Geppetto to prison. The poor old fellow did not know how to defend himself but wept and wailed like a child and said between his sobs: "Ungrateful boy! To think I tried so hard to make him a well-behaved Puppet! I should have given the matter more thought."

What happened after this is an almost unbelievable story, but you may read it in the chapters that follow.

IV

THE STORY OF PINOCCHIO AND THE TALKING CRICKET, IN WHICH ONE SEES THAT NAUGHTY CHILDREN DO NOT LIKE TO BE CORRECTED BY THOSE WISER THAN THEY ARE.

Poor old Geppetto was soon in prison. In the meantime that rascal, Pinocchio, free now from the clutches of the policeman, was running wildly across fields and meadows, taking one short cut after another towards home. In his wild flight he leaped over brambles and bushes and across brooks and ponds.

On reaching home he found the house door half open. He slipped into the room, locked the door and threw himself on the floor, happy at his escape. But his happiness lasted only a short time, for just then he heard someone saying:

"Cri-cri-cri!"

"Who is calling me?"

"I am."

Pinocchio turned and saw a large cricket crawling slowly up the wall.

"Tell me, Cricket, who are you?"

"I am the Talking Cricket and I have been living in this room for more than one than one hundred years."

"Today, however, this room is mine," said the Puppet, "and if you wish to do me a favour, get out now, and don't return.

"I refuse to leave this spot," answered the Cricket, "until I have told you a great truth."

"Tell it then, and hurry."

"Woe to boys who refuse to obey their parents and run away from home! They will never be happy in this world, and when they are older they will greatly regret it."

"Sing on, Cricket mine, as you please. Tomorrow, at dawn, I leave this place forever. If I stay here the same thing will happen to me which happens to all other boys and girls. They are sent to school, and whether they want to or not, they must study. As for me, let me tell you, I hate to study! It's much more fun, I think, to chase after butterflies, climb trees, and steal bird's nests.

"Poor foolish Puppet! Don't you realise that if you go on like that you will grow into a perfect donkey and be the laughingstock of everyone?"

"Be still, ugly Cricket!" cried Pinocchio. But the Cricket, who was a wise old philosopher, instead of being offended, continued in the same tone:

"If you do not like going to school, why don't you at least learn a trade, so that you can earn an honest living?"

"Shall I tell you something?" asked Pinocchio, who was beginning to lose patience. "Of all the trades in the world, there is only one that really suits me."

"And what can that be?"

"That of eating, drinking, sleeping, playing and wandering around from morning till night."

"Let me tell you for your own good, Pinocchio," said the Talking Cricket in his calm voice, "That those who follow that trade always end up in the hospital or in prison."

"Careful, Cricket! If you make me angry you'll be sorry!"

"Poor Pinocchio, I am sorry for you."

"Why?"

"Because you are a Puppet, and even worse, you have a wooden head."

At these last words, Pinocchio jumped up in a fury, took a wooden mallet from the bench and threw it with all his strength at the Talking Cricket. Perhaps he did not think he would actually hit it, but sad to relate, he did, right on its head. With a last weak "cri-cri-cri" the poor Cricket fell from the wall, dead!

V

PINOCCHIO IS HUNGRY AND TRIES TO COOK HIMSELF AN EGG, BUT IS SURPRISED WHEN THE OMELETTE JUMPS OUT OF THE WINDOW

If the Cricket's death scared Pinocchio at all, it was only for a very few moments. For, as night came on, a queer, empty feeling at the pit of his stomach reminded the Puppet that he had eaten nothing as yet. A boy's appetite grows very fast, and in a few moments the empty feeling had become hunger, and soon he was ravenous.

Poor Pinocchio ran to the fireplace where the pot was boiling and stretched out his hand to take the cover off, but to his amazement the pot was only painted! Think how he felt! His long nose became at least two inches longer. He ran about the room, dug in all the boxes and drawers, and even looked under the bed in search of a piece of bread, or a cookie, or perhaps a bit of fish. A bone left by a dog would have tasted good to him! But he found nothing. And meanwhile his hunger grew. The only relief poor Pinocchio had was to yawn; and his mouth stretched out to the tips of his ears. Soon he became dizzy and faint. He wept and wailed to himself: "The Talking Cricket was right. It was wrong of me to disobey Father and to run away from home. Oh, how horrible it is to be hungry!"

Suddenly he saw, amongst the sweepings in a corner, something round and white. In a jiffy he pounced upon it. It was an egg. The Puppet's joy knew no bounds. He turned the egg over and over in his hands, fondled and kissed and talked to it: "And now, how shall I cook you? Shall I make an omelette? No, it is better to fry you in a pan! Or shall I drink you? No, the best way is to fry you, you will taste better." No sooner said than done. He placed a little pan over a warmer full of hot coals. In the pan he poured a little water. As soon as the water started to boil he broke the eggshell, but in place of the white and yolk of the egg, a little fluffy yellow chick escaped from it. Bowing politely to Pinocchio, he said to him: "Many thanks indeed for having saved me the trouble of breaking my shell! Good-bye and good luck to you!" With these words it hopped up on the window ledge and darted away.

The poor Puppet stood as if turned to stone, with wide eyes, open mouth and the empty halves of the eggshell in his hands. When he came to himself, he began to cry and shrieked at the top of his voice, stamping his feet on the ground and wailing: "The Talking Cricket was right! If I had not run away from home and if Father were here now, I should not be dying of hunger. And as his stomach kept grumbling and he had nothing to quiet it with, he thought of going out to the near-by village in the hope of finding some kind person who might give him a bit of bread.

PINOCCHIO FALLS ASLEEP WITH HIS FEET ON A FOOT WARMER, AND WHEN HE WAKES UP HE HAS NO FEET.

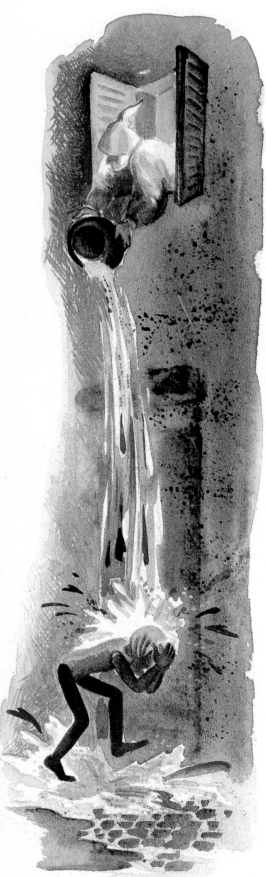

Pinocchio hated the dark street, but he was so hungry that in spite of this, he ran out of the house. The night was pitch black. It thundered and bright flashes of lightning now and again shot across the sky, turning it into a sea of fire.

Pinocchio was greatly afraid of thunder and lightning, but the hunger he felt was far greater than his fear. The whole village was dark and deserted. The doors and windows of all the stores were closed. In the streets, not even a dog could be seen.

Pinocchio, in desperation, ran up to a doorway, threw himself upon the bell and pulled it wildly, saying to himself: "Someone will surely answer that!" He was right. An old man in a nightcap opened the window and looked out. He called down angrily: "What do you want at this hour of night?" "Will you be good enough to give me a bit of bread? I am hungry." "Wait a minute and I'll come right back," answered the old fellow, thinking he had to deal with one of those boys who love to roam around at night ringing people's bells while they are asleep.

After a minute or two the same voice cried: "Get under the window and hold out your hat!" Pinocchio had no hat, but he managed to get under the window just in time to feel a shower of ice-cold water pour down on his poor wooden head and shoulders and over his whole body. He returned home soaking wet, weary and hungry.

As he no longer had any strength to stand, he sat down on a little stool and put his two feet on the stove to dry them. There he fell asleep, and while he slept, his wooden feet began to burn. Slowly, very slowly, they blackened and turned to ashes.

GEPPETTO RETURNS HOME AND GIVES HIS OWN BREAKFAST TO THE PUPPET.

Pinocchio slept deeply and snored, because he could not feel his wooden feet burning. Then there was a loud knocking on the door. "It is I, called Geppetto, let me in." The poor Puppet, who was still half asleep, had not yet found out that his two feet were burned and gone. As soon as he heard his Father's voice, he jumped up to open the door but fell headlong to the floor. "Open the door for me!" Geppetto shouted from the street."

"Father, dear Father, I can't," answered the Puppet in despair, crying and rolling on the floor.

"Why can't you?"

"Because someone has eaten my feet."

"And who has eaten them?"

"The cat," answered Pinocchio, seeing that little animal busily playing with some shavings in the corner of the room.

"Open! I say," repeated Geppetto; "or I'll give you a sound whipping when I get in."

"Father, believe me, I can't stand up. Oh, dear! Oh, dear! I shall have to walk on my knees all my life.

Gepetto, thinking that all these tears and cries were only the Puppet's tricks, climbed up the side of the house and went in through the window. At first he was very angry, but on seeing Pinocchio stretched out on the floor and really without feet, he felt sorry, and picking him up from the floor, he hugged him close and said:

"My dear little Pinocchio, how did you burn your feet?"

"I don't know, Father, but it has been a terrible night, I shall never forget it as long as I live. There was noisy thunder and very bright lightning — and I was so hungry. And then the Talking Cricket told me I deserved it, because I was bad, and I said to him 'Careful Cricket', and he said to me 'You are a Puppet and you have a wooden head'; and I threw the mallet at him and killed him. It was his own fault, for I didn't want to kill him. And I put the pan on the coals to cook an egg I found, but a chicken came out of it and ran away.

And my hunger grew, and I went out to see if anyone would give me some food, and an old man with a nightcap looked out of the window and threw water on me, and I came home and put my feet on the stove to dry them, and fell asleep and now my feet are gone but my hunger isn't! And poor Pinocchio began to scream and cry so loudly that he could be heard for miles around.

Geppetto, who had understood nothing of all that jumbled talk, except that the Puppet was hungry, felt sorry for him and, pulling three pears out of his pocket, offered them to him, saying: "These three pears were for my breakfast, but I give them to you gladly. Eat them now and stop crying."

"If you want me to eat them, please peel them for me."

"Peel them?" asked Geppetto, very surprised. "I should never have throught that you were so dainty and fussy about your food. That's too bad. Even children should be taught to eat everything that is given to them, for we never know what life holds in store for us, and if we are too particular we may have to go hungry.

"Well, I will not eat the pears if they are not peeled. I don't like them." And good old Geppetto took out a knife, peeled the three pears and put the skins in a row on the corner of the table.

Pinoccho ate one pear quickly and started to throw the core away, but Geppetto held his arm, saying:

"Oh, no, don't throw it away! Everything in the world may be of some use!"

"But the core I will not eat!" cried Pinocchio in an angry tone.

"Who knows?" repeated Geppetto calmly; and the three cores were soon placed on the table next to the skins. Pinocchio had eaten the three pears, or rather devoured them. Then he yawned deeply and waited:

"I'm still hungry."

"I have no more to give you."

"Really, nothing at all?"

"Only these three cores and the skins."

"Very well, then," said Pinocchio, "if there is nothing else I'll eat them." At first he made a wry face, but one after another, the skins and the cores disappeared.

"Oh! Now I feel fine!" he said, after eating the last one.

"You see," observed Geppetto, "that I was right when I told you that one must not be too fussy and too dainty about food. We never know what the future holds for us!"

GEPPETTO MAKES PINOCCHIO A NEW
PAIR OF FEET, AND SELLS HIS COAT
TO BUY HIM A SCHOOL BOOK.

The Puppet, as soon as his hunger was appeased, started to grumble and cry that he wanted a new pair of feet. But Master Geppetto, in order to punish him for his mischief, left him alone the whole morning. After dinner he said to him: "Why should I remake your feet — to allow you run away from home again?

"I promise you," answered the Puppet, sobbing, "that from now on I'll be good."

"Boys always promise that when they want something." said Geppetto.

"I promise to go to school every day, to study and to pass all my examinations."

"Boys always sing that song when they want their own way."

"But I am not like other boys! I am better than all of them and I always tell the truth. I promise you, Father, that I'll learn a trade and I'll be the comfort of your old age."

Geppetto, though trying to look very stern, felt his heart soften when he saw Pinocchio so unhappy. He said no more, but taking his tools and two pieces of wood, set to work and in less than an hour the feet were finished; two slender, nimble little feet, strong and quick.

"Close your eyes and sleep!" Geppetto then said and Pinocchio closed his eyes and pretended to be asleep while Geppo stuck on the two feet, doing his work so well that the joint could hardly be seen.

As soon as the Puppet felt his new feet he gave one leap from the table and started to skip and jump around from very joy. "To show you how grateful I am to you Father, I'll go to school right now, but I shall need a suit of clothes."

Geppetto did not have a penny in his pocket, so he made his son a little suit of flowered paper, a pair of shoes from the bark of a tree, and a tiny cap from a bit of dough. Pinocchio ran to look at his reflection in a bowl of water, and he felt so happy that he said proudly: "Now I look like a gentleman." "Maybe, replied Geppetto, but remember that fine clothes do not make a fine man." "That may be true replied Pinocchio, but there is one important requirement for school that we have overlooked."
"What is it?"
"An A-B-C book."
"To be sure! But how shall we get it?"
"That's easy. We'll go to a book store and buy it."

"And the money?"
"We have none, "said the old man, sadly.

Pinocchio did not reply, although he was usually happy, he was beginning to realise that poverty was a very serious and unpleasant state.

"What does it matter, after all?" cried Geppetto all at once, as he jumped up from his chair. Putting on his old coat, full of darns and patches, he left the house without another word.

After a while he returned. In his hands he had the A-B-C book for his son, but the old coat was gone. The poor fellow was in his shirt sleeves and the day was cold.
"Where's your coat, Father?"
"I have sold it,"
"Why did you sell your coat?"
"It was too warm."
But Pinocchio understood the answer, and unable to restrain his tears, he kissed his Father over and over again.

PINOCCHIO SELLS HIS SCHOOL BOOK
TO ENTER THE PUPPET THEATRE.

A short time later Pinocchio was hurrying off to school with his new A-B-C book under his arm! As he walked along his brain was busy planning hundreds of wonderful things. Talking to himself, he said: "In school today, I'll learn to read, tomorrow to write, and the day after tomorrow I'll do arithmetic. Then, clever as I am, I can earn a lot of money. With the very first money I make, I'll buy Father a new cloth coat. No, not just cloth — it shall be of gold and silver with diamond buttons. That dear man certainly deserves it, for he is now without a coat and in his shirt sleeves because he was good enough to buy my school primer for me. On this cold day, too!

As he talked to himself, he thought he heard sounds of pipes and drums coming from a distance: He stopped to listen. Those sounds came from a little street that led to a small village along the shore. "What can that noise be? What a nuisance that I have to go to school! Otherwise ...." Then he stopped and thought. He felt he had to make up his mind for either one thing or the other — should he go to school, or should he follow the pipes? He reached a decision — "Today I'll follow the pipes and tomorrow I'll go to school. There's always plenty of time to go to school." decided the little rascal at last, shrugging his shoulders. No sooner said than done. He started quickly down the street. On he ran and louder grew the sounds of pipe and drum....

Suddenly, he found himself in a large square, full of people standing in front of a little wooden building painted in brilliant colours.
"What is that house?" Pinocchio asked a little boy standing near him.
"Read the sign and you'll know."
"I'd like to read, but somehow I can't today."
"Then I'll read it to you. Know then, Ninny, that written in letters of fire I see the words: GREAT PUPPET THEATRE."
"When does the show start?"
"It's starting now."
"And how much does one pay to get in?"
"Four cents."

Pinocchio, who was wild with curiosity to know what was going on inside, lost all his pride and said to the boy shamelessly:

"Will you give me four cents until tomorrow?"

"I'd give them to you gladly," answered the other with a grin, "but somehow I can't today."

"I'll sell my coat for four cents."

"What would I do with a coat of flowered paper if it rained?"

"Do you want to buy my shoes?"

"They are only good enough to light a fire with."

"What about my hat!"

"A fine bargain indeed! A cap of dough! The mice might come and eat it from my head!"

Pinocchio was almost in tears. He was just about to make one last offer, but lacked the courage to do so. He hesitated, he could not make up his mind. At last he said:

"Will you give me four cents for the book?"

"I am a boy and I buy nothing from boys." said the little fellow with far more common sense than the Puppet had shown.

"I'll give you four cents for your School book," said a second-hand dealer who stood by. Then and there, the book changed hands. And poor old Geppetto sat at home in his shirt sleeves, shivering with cold, having sold his coat to buy that little book for the Puppet.

X

THE PUPPETS RECOGNIZE THEIR BROTHER PINOCCHIO, AND WELCOME HIM WITH LOUD CHEERS, BUT THE DIRECTOR 'FIRE EATER' NEEDS HIM FOR FIREWOOD.

Pinocchio was very excited when he at last entered the Puppet Theatre. The curtain was up and the performance had started. Harlequin and Pulcinella were on the stage and, as usual, they were threatening each other with sticks and blows. The audience were enjoying the spectacle and laughing at the antics of the puppets behaving just like real people.

The play continued for a few minutes and then, suddenly, Harlequin stopped talking. Turning towards the audience, he pointed to the rear of the theatre yelling loudly "Look, look! Do I really see Pinocchio there?"

"Yes, yes! It is Pinocchio!" screamed Pulcinella.

"It is! It is!" shrieked Miss Rosa, peeking in from the side of the stage.

"It is Pinocchio! yelled all the Puppets pouring out of the wings. It is our brother Pinocchio! Hurrah for Pinocchio!"

"Pinocchio come up here to me," shouted Harlequin. "Come to the arms of your wooden brothers!"

At such a loving invitation Pinocchio, with one leap from the back of the theatre found himself in the front rows. With another leap, he was on the orchestra leader's head. With a third, he landed on the stage. It is impossible to describe the shrieks of joy, the warm embraces and the friendly greetings with which the strange company of dramatic actors received Pinocchio. It was a touching scene, but the audience, seeing that the play had stopped, became angry and began to yell: "The play, the play, we want the play!" However instead of going on with their act, the Puppets made twice as much noise and, lifting Pinocchio up onto their shoulders, carried him around the stage in triumph!

At that very moment, the Theatre Director came out of his room. He had such a fearful appearance that one look at him would fill you with horror. His beard was as black as pitch, and so long that it reached from his chin down to his feet. His mouth was as wide as an oven, his teeth like yellow fangs, and his eyes, two glowing red coals. In his huge, hairy hands, a long whip, made of green snakes and black cats' tails twisted together, swished through the air in a dangerous way. At the unexpected apparition, no one dared even to breathe. One could almost hear a fly go by. Those poor Puppets, one and all, trembled like leaves in a storm.
"Why have you disturbed my players? " the huge fellow asked Pinocchio with the voice of an ogre suffering with a cold.
"Believe me, your Honour, the fault was not mine."
"Enough! Be quiet! I'll take care of you later."

As soon as the play was over, the Director went to the kitchen, where a fine big lamb was slowly turning on the spit. More wood was needed to finish cooking it. He called Harlequin and Pulcinella and said to them: "Bring that Puppet to me! He looks as if he were made of well-seasoned wood. He' ll make a fine fire for this spit."

Harlequin and Pulcinella hesitated, then frightened by a look from their master, they left the kitchen to obey him. A few minutes later they returned, carrying poor Pinocchio, who was wriggling and squirming like an eel and crying pitifully: "Father, save me! I don't want to die! I don't want to die!"

XI

'FIRE EATER' SNEEZES AND FORGIVES PINOCCHIO, WHO SAVES HIS FRIEND HARLEQUIN FROM DEATH.

There was great excitement in the theatre. The Director, Fire Eater - this was really his name! − was very ugly, but he was far from being as bad as he looked. Proof of this is that, when he saw the poor Puppet being brought in to him, struggling with fear and crying: "I don't want to die! I don't want to die!" he felt sorry for him and began first to waver and then to weaken. Finally he could control himself no longer and gave a loud sneeze. At that sneeze, Harlequin, who until then had been as sad and worried, smiled happily and leaning toward the Puppet, whispered "Good news, Pinocchio! Fire Eater has sneezed and this means that he feels sorry for you. You are saved! For while other people cry when they are sad, Fire Eater has the strange habit of sneezing each time he feels unhappy and this shows the kindness of his heart!"

After sneezing, Fire Eater, ugly as ever, cried to Pinocchio: "Stop crying! Your wails give me a funny feeling down here in my stomach and..." two loud sneezes finished his speech.
"God bless you!" said Pinocchio.
"Thanks! Are your father and mother still living? demanded Fire Eater.
"My father, yes. My mother I have never known."

"Your poor father would suffer terribly if I were to use you as fire wood. Poor old man! I feel so sorry for him!" Three more sneezes followed, louder than ever.

"God bless you!" repeated Pinocchio.

"Thanks! However, I ought to be sorry for myself too, just now. My good dinner is spoiled. I have no more wood for the fire and the lamb is only half cooked. Never mind! In your place I'll burn some other Puppet. Hey there! Officers!

At the call, two wooden officers appeared, long and thin, with queer hats on their heads and swords in their hands. Fire Eater yelled at them in a hoarse voice:

"Take Harlequin, tie him and throw him on the fire. I want my lamb well done!"

Think of how poor Harlequin felt! He was so scared that his legs doubled up under him and he fell to the floor. Pinocchio, at that heartbreaking sight, threw himself at the feet of Fire Eater and, weeping bitterly, asking in a pitiful voice which could scarcely be heard:

"Have pity, I beg of you, Sir."

"There are no sirs here!"

"Have pity, kind Sir!"

"There are no kind sirs here!"

"Have pity, your Excellency!"

On hearing himself addressed as your Excellency, the director of the Puppet Theatre sat up very straight in his chair, stroked his long beard, and becoming suddenly kind and compassionate, smiled proudly as he said to Pinocchio: "Well, what do you want from me now, Puppet?"

"I beg for mercy for my poor friend Harlequin, who has never done the least harm in his life."

"There is no mercy here, Pinocchio. I have spared you. Harlequin must burn in your place. I am hungry and my dinner must be cooked."

"In that case," said Pinocchio proudly, as he stood up and flung away his cap of dough, "in that case, my duty is clear. Come, officers! Tie me up and throw me on those flames. No, it is not fair that poor Harlequin, the best friend I have in the world, should die in my place!"

These brave words, said in a piecing voice, made all the other Puppets cry. Even the officers, who were made of wood also. Fire Eater at first remained hard and cold as a piece of ice; but then, little by little he softened and began to sneeze. And after four or five sneezes, he opened wide his arms and said to Pinocchio: "You are a brave boy! Come to my arms and kiss me!" Pinocchio ran to him and scurrying like a squirrel up the long black beard, he gave Fire Eater a loving kiss on the tip of his nose.

"Has pardon been granted to me?" asked poor Harlequin with a voice that was hardly a breath.

"Pardon is yours!" answered Fire Eater; and sighing and wagging his head, he added. "Well, tonight I shall have to eat my lamb only half cooked, but beware the next time Puppets."

At the news that pardon had been given, the Puppets ran to the stage and turning on all the lights, they danced and sang till dawn.

'FIRE EATER' GIVES PINOCCHIO FIVE GOLD PIECES FOR HIS FATHER GEPP-ETTO, BUT THE PUPPET MEETS A FOX AND A CAT AND FOLLOWS THEM.

The next day Fire Eater called Pinocchio aside and asked him:

"What is your father's name?"

"Geppetto."

"And what is his trade?"

"He's a wood carver."

"Does he earn much?"

"He earns so little that he never has a penny in his pockets. Just think that, in order to buy me an A-B-C book for school, he had to sell the only coat he owned, and that was full of darns and patches."

"Poor fellow! I feel sorry for him. Here, take these five gold pieces. Go give them to him with my kindest regards."

Pinocchio, as you may imagine, thanked him many times. He kissed each Puppet in turn, even the officers, and beside himself with joy, set out on his homeward journay.

He had gone barely half a mile when he met a lame Fox and a blind Cat, walking together like two good friends. The lame Fox leaned on the Cat, and the blind Cat let the Fox lead him along.

"Good morning, Pinocchio" said the Fox, greeting him courteously.

"How do you know my name?" asked the Puppet.

"I know your father well."

"Where have you seen him?"

"I saw him yesterday standing at the door of his house."

"And what was he doing?"

"He was in his shirt sleeves trembling with cold."

"Poor Father! But, after today, God willing, he will suffer no longer."

"Why?"

"Because I have become a rich man."

"You, a rich man?" said the Fox, and he began to laugh out loud. The Cat was laughing but tried to hide it by stroking his long whiskers.

"There is nothing to laugh at," cried Pinocchio angrily. "I am very sorry to make your mouth water, but these are five new gold pieces." And he pulled out the gold pieces which Fire Eater had given him.

At the cheerful tinkle of the gold, the Fox unconsciously held out his paw that was supposed to be lame, and the Cat opened wide his two eyes till they looked like live coals, but he closed them again so quickly that Pinocchio did not notice.

"And may I ask," enquired the Fox, "what you are going to do with all that money?"

"First of all," answered the Puppet, I want to buy a fine new coat for my father, a coat of gold and silver with diamond buttons; after that, I'll buy an A-B-C book for myself."

"For yourself?"

"For myself. I want to go to school and study hard."

"Look at me," said the Fox. "Because I was silly enough to want to study, I lost a paw."

"Look at me," said the Cat. "For the same foolish reason, I have lost the sight of both eyes."

At that very moment a blackbird, perched on the fence by the road, called out sharp and clear: "Pinocchio, do not listen to bad advice. If you do, you'll be sorry!"
Poor little blackbird! If he had only kept his words to himself! At that very moment the cat leaped on him and ate him, feathers and all. After eating the bird, he cleaned his whiskers, closed his eyes, and appeared blind once again.
"Why did you kill the blackbird?"
"I wanted to teach him a lesson, he talked too much."

By this time the three companions had walked a long distance. Suddenly, the Fox stopped in his tracks and turning to the Puppet, said to him:
"Do you want to double your gold pieces?"
"What do you mean?"
"Do you want one hundred, a thousand, two thousand gold pieces for your miserable five?"
"Yes, but how could I do that?"
"The way is very easy. Instead of returning home, come with us."
"And where will you take me?"
"To the city of Simple Simons."
Pinocchio thought a while and then said firmly:
"No, I don't want to go. Home is near, and my father will be waiting for me. How unhappy he must be that I have not yet returned! I have been a bad son, and the Talking Cricket was right when he said that a disobedient boy cannot be happy in this world. I have learned this lesson at my own expense. Even last night in the theatre, when Fire Eater .... the shivers run up and down my back at the very thought of it."
"Well then," said the Fox, "if you really want to go home, go ahead, but you'll be sorry!"
"You'll be sorry," repeated the Cat.
"Think well, Pinocchio, you are turning your back on Dame Fortune."
"On Dame Fortune," repeated the Cat.

"Tomorrow your five gold pieces will be two thousand."

"But how can they possibly become so many?" asked Pinocchio wonderingly.

"I'll explain," said the Fox. "You must know that, just outside the city of Simple Simons there is a blessed field called the Field of Wonders. In this field you dig a hole and in the hole you bury a gold piece. After covering up the hole with earth you water it well, sprinkle a bit of salt on it, and go to bed. During the night, the gold piece sprouts, grows, blossoms and next morning you find a beautiful tree, loaded with gold pieces."

"So that if I were to bury my five gold pieces," cried Pinocchio with growing interest, "next morning I should find - how many?"

"It is very simple to figure out," answered the Fox. "Why, you can figure it on your fingers! Granted that each piece gives you five hundred, multiply five hundred by five. Next morning you will find twenty-five hundred new, sparkling gold pieces."

"Fine! Fine! cried Pinocchio, dancing with joy. "And as soon as I have them I shall keep two thousand for myself and the other five hundred I'll give to you two."

"A gift for us?" cried the Fox, pretending to be insulted. "Why of course not!"

"Of course not" repeated the Cat.

"We do not work for gain," answered the Fox. "We work only to enrich others."

"To enrich others!" repeated the Cat.

"What good people," thought Pinocchio to himself. And, forgetting his father, the new coat, the Primary School book and all his good resolutions, he said to the Fox and the Cat:

"Let us go, I am with you."

XIII

AT THE INN OF THE RED LOBSTER

Cat, Fox and Puppet walked and walked. At last, toward evening, dead tired, they came to the Inn of the Red Lobster. "Let us stop here awhile," said the Fox, "to eat a bite and rest for a few hours. At midnight we'll start out again, for at dawn tomorrow we must be at the Field of Wonders." They went into the Inn and sat down at a table. However, not one of them was very hungry.

The poor Cat felt very weak, and he was able to eat only thirty-five mullet with tomato sauce and four portions of tripe with cheese. Moreover, as he was so in need of strength he had to have four more helpings of butter and cheese. The Fox had to be coaxed to eat a little. The doctor had put him on a diet and he could only manage to eat a small hare dressed with a dozen young spring chickens, followed by some partridges, a few pheasants, a couple of rabbits, and a dozen frogs and lizards. That was all. He felt ill, he said, and could not eat another bite. Pinocchio ate least of all. He asked for a slice of bread and some nuts and then hardly touched them. The poor lad, with his mind on the Field of Wonders, was suffering from gold-piece indigestion!

Supper over, the Fox said to the Innkeeper: "Give us two good rooms, one for Mr Pinocchio and the other for my friend and myself; we will take a little nap, but remember to call us at midnight sharp, for we must continue on our journey."

"Yes, sir," answered the Innkeeper, winking in a knowing way at the Fox and Cat, as if to say, "I understand."

As soon as Pinocchio was in bed, he fell fast asleep and began to dream. He dreamed he was in the middle of a field. The field was full of vines heavy with grapes. The grapes were no other than gold coins, which tinkled merrily as they swayed in the wind. They seemed to say "Let him who wants us take us!" Just as Pinocchio stretched out his hand to take a handful of them, he was awakened by three loud knocks at the door. It was the Innkeeper who had come to tell him that midnight had struck.

"Are my friends ready?" the Puppet asked him.

"Indeed, yes! They went two hours ago."

"Why in such a hurry?"

"Unfortunately the Cat received a telegram which said that his first-born was suffering from chillblains and on the point of death. He could not even wait to say good-bye to you."

"Did they pay for the supper?"

"How could they do such a thing?" Being people of great refinement, they did not want to offend you as not to allow you the honour of paying the bill."

"Too bad! That offense would have been more than pleasing to me." said Pinocchio.

"Where did my good friends say they would wait for me?" he added.

"At the Field of Wonders, at sunrise tomorrow morning."

31

Pinocchio paid a gold piece for the three suppers and started on his way toward the field that was to make him a rich man. He walked on, not knowing where he was going, for it was dark and not a thing was visible. Not a leaf stirred. A few bats skimmed his nose now and then and scared him greatly. Once or twice he shouted: "Who goes there?" and the far off hills echoed back "Who goes there?" "Who goes there?"

As he walked, Pinocchio noticed a tiny insect glimmering on the trunk of a tree, a small being that glowed with a pale, soft light.

"Who are you?" he asked.

"I am the ghost of the Talking Cricket." answered the little being in a faint voice that sounded as if it came from a far-away world.

"What do you want?" asked the Puppet.

"I want to give you a few words of advice. Return home and give the four gold pieces you have left to your poor old father who is weeping because he has not seen you for so long."

"Tomorrow my father will be a rich man, for these four gold pieces will become two thousand."

"Don't listen to those who promise you wealth overnight. As a rule they are either fools or swindlers! Listen to me and go home."

"But I want to go on!"

"The night is very dark."

"I want to go on."

"The road is dangerous."

"I still want to go on."

"Remember that boys who insist on having their own way, and ignore good advice, sooner or later suffer for it."

"The same old nonsense. Good-bye Cricket."

"Good night, Pinocchio, and may Heaven preserve you from the assassins."

There was silence for a minute and the light of the Talking Cricket disappeared suddenly, just as if someone had snuffed it out. Once again the road was plunged into darkness.

XIV

PINOCCHIO DOES NOT LISTEN TO THE GOOD ADVICE OF THE TALKING CRICKET AND FALLS INTO THE HANDS OF THE ASSASSINS.

"When I come to think of it," said the Puppet to himself, as he once more set out on his journey, "we boys are really very unlucky. Everybody scolds us, everybody gives us advice, everybody warns us. If we were to allow it, everyone would try to be father and mother to us; — even the talking cricket! Just because I would not listen to that pesky cricket, who knows how many misfortunes are supposed to be awaiting me! Assassins indeed! At least I have never believed in them, nor ever will. I think assassins have been invented by fathers and mothers to frighten children. And then, even if I were to meet them on the road, what matter? I'll just run up to them and say: Well Sirs, what do you want? "You can't fool with me! Run along and mind your own business." I can almost see those

fellows running like the wind. But in case they don't run, I can always run myself ..."
Pinocchio was not given time to talk to himself any longer, for he thought he heard a slight
rustle among the leaves behind him. He turned to look and behold, there in the darkness
stood two big black shadows, wrapped from head to foot in black sacks. The two figures
leaped toward him as softly as if they were ghosts.

"Here they come!" Pinocchio said to himself, and not knowing where to hide the
gold pieces, he stuck all four of them under his tongue. He tried to run away, but hardly had
he taken a step when he felt his arms grasped and heard two horrible, deep voices say "Your
money or your life!" On account of the gold pieces in his mouth Pinocchio could not say a
word, so he tried with head and hands to show, as best he could that he was only a poor
Puppet without a penny in his pocket.

"Come, come, less nonsense, and out with your money!" cried the two thieves
in threatening voices. Once more Pinocchio's head and hands said, "I haven't a penny."
"Out with that money or you're a dead man," said the taller of the two assassins.
"Dead man," repeated the other.
"And after having killed you, we will kill your father also."
"Your father also."
"No, No, not my father!" cried Pinocchio, terrified, but as he screamed, the gold pieces
tinkled together in. his mouth. "Ah, you rascal! So that's the game! You have the money
hidden under your tongue. Out with it!" But Pinocchio was as stubborn as ever.
"Are you deaf? Wait, young man, we'll get it from you, whether you like it or not!"

One of them grabbed the Puppet by the nose and the other by the chin, and they
pulled him unmercifully from side to side in order to make him open his mouth, without
success. The Puppet's lips might as well have been nailed together. They would not open. In

desperation the smaller of the two assassins pulled out a long knife from his pocket and tried to pry Pinocchio's mouth open with it. Quick as a flash, the Puppet sank his teeth deep into the assassin's hand, bit it off and spat it out. Imagine his surprise when he saw that it was not a hand, but a cat's paw.

Encouraged by this first victory, he freed himself from the claws of his assailants and leaping over the bushes along the road, ran swiftly across the fields. His pursuers were after him at once, like dogs chasing a hare.

After running several miles, Pinocchio was almost exhausted. Seeing he was lost, he climbed up a giant pine tree and sat there, looking around. The assassins arrived and tried to climb up also, but slipped and fell back. Far from giving up the chase, however, this only spurred them on to greater activity. They gathered wood and piled it up at the foot of the pine, then set fire to it. The tree began to sputter and burn like a chandle blown by the wind. As the flames climbed higher and higher, Pinocchio jumped quickly to the ground and ran, the assassins close to him as before.

Dawn was breaking when, without any warning, Pinocchio found his path barred by a deep pool full of water the colour of muddy coffee. With a "One, two, three!" he jumped right across it. The assassins jumped also, but not having measured their distance well — splash!!! — they fell right into the middle of the pool. Pinocchio, who heard the splash, laughed aloud, but never stopped running. He thought they must surely be drowned and turned his head to see. But there were the two sombre figures still following him, although their black sacks were drenched and dripping with water.

XV

THE ASSASSINS CHASE PINOCCHIO, CATCH HIM AND HANG HIM TO THE BRANCH OF A GIANT OAK TREE.

As he ran, the Puppet felt more and more certain that he would have to give himself up into the hands of his pursuers. Suddenly he saw a little cottage gleaming white as snow among the trees. "If I have enough breath left with which to reach that little house I may be saved." he said to himself, and darted swiftly through the woods. The Assassins still after him.

After a hard race of almost an hour, tired and out of breath, Pinocchio finally reached the door of the cottage and knocked. No one answered. He knocked again, harder than before, for behind him he heard the steps and laboured breathing of his persecutors. The same silence followed. As knocking was of no use, Pinocchio in despair began to kick and bang against the door as if he wanted to break it in. At the noise, a window opened and a lovely young girl looked out. She had azure hair and a face white as wax. Her eyes were closed and her hands crossed on her breast. With a voice so weak that it could hardly be heard, she whispered:
"No one lives in this house. Everyone is dead."
"Won't you, at least, open the door for me?" cried Pinocchio in a beseeching voice.
"I also am dead."

"Dead? What are you doing at the window then?"

"I am waiting for the coffin to take me away."

After these words, the maiden disappeared and the window closed without a sound.

"Oh, Lovely Maiden with Azure Hair," cried Pinocchio, "open, I beg of you. Take pity on a poor boy who is being chased by two Assass...." He did not finish, for two powerful hands grasped him by the neck and the same two horrible voices growled threateningly: "Now we have you!" The Puppet, seeing death dancing before him, trembled so hard that the joints of his legs rattled and the coins tinkled under his tongue.

"Well, the Assassins asked "will you open your mouth now or not? Ah! you do not answer? Very well, this time you shall open it." Taking out two long, sharp knives they struck two heavy blows on the Puppet's back. Happily for him, Pinocchio was made of very hard wood and the knives broke into pieces. The Assassins looked at each other in dismay, holding the handles of the knives in their hands. "I see" said one to the other, "there is nothing left to do now but to hang him."

"To hang him," repeated the other.

They tied Pinocchio's hands behind his back and slipped the noose around his neck. Throwing the rope over the high limb of a giant oak tree, they pulled till the poor Puppet hung far up in space. Satisfied with their work, they sat on the grass waiting for Pinocchio to give his last gasp. But after three hours the Puppet's eyes were still open, his mouth still shut, and his legs kicked harder than ever.

Tired of waiting, the Assassins called to him mockingly: "Good-bye till tomorrow. When we return in the morning we hope you'll be polite enough to let us find you dead and gone and with your mouth wide open." With these words they went.

A few minutes went by and then a wild wind started to blow. As it shrieked and moaned, the poor little sufferer was blown to and fro like the hammer of a bell. The rocking made him seasick and the noose, becoming tighter and tighter, choked him. Little by little a film covered his eyes.

Death was creeping nearer and the Puppet still hoped for someone to come to his rescue, but no one appeared. As he was about to die, he thought of his poor old Father, and hardly conscious of what he was saying, murmered to himself: "Oh, Father, dear Father! If you were only here!" These were his last words. He closed his eyes, opened his mouth, stretched out his legs, and hung there, as if he were dead.

XVI

THE LOVELY MAIDEN WITH AZURE HAIR SENDS FOR THE POOR PUPPET, PUTS HIM TO BED AND CALLS THREE DOCTORS TO TELL HER IF PINOCCHIO IS DEAD OR ALIVE.

If the poor Puppet had dangled there much longer, all hope would have been lost. Luckily for him, the Lovely Maiden with Azure Hair once again looked out of her window. Filled with pity at the sight of the poor little fellow being knocked helplessly about by the wind, she clapped her hands sharply three times.

At the signal a loud whirr of wings in quick flight was heard and a large Falcon came and settled on the window ledge.
"What do you command, my charming Fairy?" asked the Falcon, bending its beak in deep reverence (for it must be known that the Lovely Maiden with Azure Hair was none other than a very kind Fairy who had lived for more than a thousand years near the forest.)
"Do you see that Puppet hanging from the limb of the giant oak tree?":
"I see him."
"Very well. Fly now to him and with your strong beak break the knot which holds him tied, take him down and lay him softly on the grass at the foot of the oak." The Falcon flew away and after two minutes returned, saying:
"I have done what you commanded."
"How did you find him? Alive or dead?"
"At first glance, I thought he was dead, but I was wrong, for a soon as I loosened the knot around his neck, he gave a long sigh and mumbled "Now I feel better!""

The Fairy clapped her hands twice. A magnificent Poodle appeared, walking on his hind legs just like a man. He was dressed in court livery. A three cornered hat trimmed with gold lace was set at a rakish angle over a wig of white curls that dropped down to his waist. He wore a jaunty coat of chocolate-coloured velvet, with diamond buttons, and with two huge pockets which were always filled with bones, dropped there at dinner by his loving mistress. Breeches of crimson velvet, silk stockings and low silver buckles completed his costume.

"Come, Medoro" said the Fairy to him. "Get my best coach ready and go to the

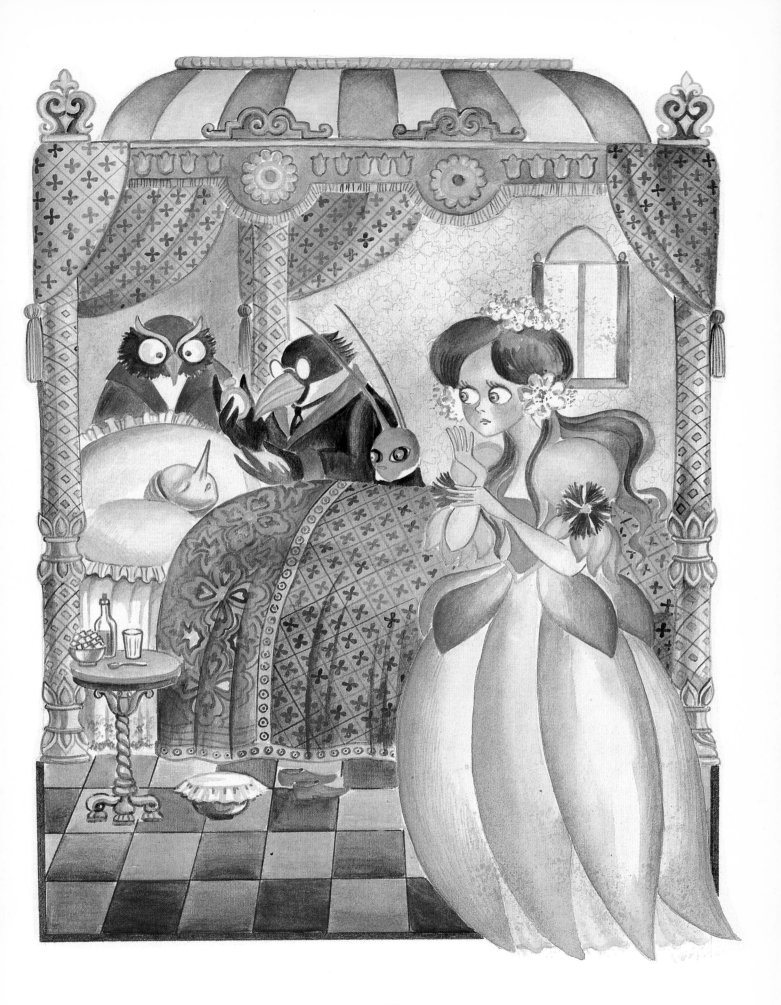

forest. At the giant oak tree you will find a poor half-dead Puppet stretched out on the grass. Lift him up gently, place him on the silken cushions of the coach and bring him to me." The Poodle set off at a quick pace.

In a few minutes a lovely little coach, made of glass, with lining as soft as whipped cream and chocolate pudding, and stuffed with canary feathers, pulled out of the stable. It was drawn by one hundred pairs of white mice. The Poodle sat on the coachmen's seat and snapped his whip gaily in the air. In a quarter of an hour the coach was back. The Fairy, who was waiting at the door of the house, lifted the poor little Puppet in her arms, took him to a dainty room with mother-of-pearl walls, put him to bed and sent immediately for the most famous doctors of the neighbourhood to come to her.

One after another the doctors came, a Crow, an Owl and a Talking Cricket. "I should like to know if this poor Puppet is dead or alive." said the Fairy. At this invitation the Crow stepped out and felt Pinocchio's pulse, his nose, his little toe. Then he solemnly pronounced the following words: "To my mind this Puppet is dead and gone; but if by any chance, he were not, then that would be a sure sign that he is still alive!"
"I am sorry," said the Owl, "to have to contradict the Crow, my famous friend and colleague. To my mind this Puppet is alive; but if, by any chance, he were not, then that would be a sure sign that he is wholly dead!"
"And do you hold any opinion?" the Fairy asked the Talking Cricket.
"I say that a wise doctor, when he does not know what he is talking about, should know enough to keep his mouth shut. However, that Puppet is not a stranger to me. I have known him a long time!" Pinocchio, who until then had been very quiet, shuddered so hard that the bed shook. "He is a rascal of the worst kind, a rude, lazy runaway, and a disobedient son who is breaking his father's heart."

Long shuddering sobs were heard, cries and deep sighs.
"When the dead weep, they are beginning to recover," said the Crow solemnly.
"I am sorry to contradict my famous friend and colleague," said the Crow, "but as far as I'm concerned, I think that when the dead weep, it means they do not want to die!"

XVII

PINOCCHIO EATS SUGAR, BUT REFUSES TO TAKE MEDICINE. WHEN THE UNDERTAKERS COME FOR HIM, HE DRINKS THE MEDICINE AND FEELS BETTER. LATER HE TELLS A LIE AND, IN PUNISHMENT, HIS NOSE GROWS LONGER AND LONGER.

As soon as the doctors had left the room, the Fairy went to Pinocchio's bed and, touching him on the forehead, noticed he was burning with fever. She took a glass of water, put a white powder into it, and handing it to the Puppet, said lovingly to him "drink this, and in a few days you'll be up and well." Pinocchio looked at the glass, made a wry face and asked in a whining voice:
"Is it sweet or bitter?"
"It is bitter, but it is good for you."
"If it is bitter, I don't want it."
"Drink it!"

"I don't like anything bitter."

"Drink it and I'll give you a lump of sugar to take the bitter taste from your mouth."

"Where's the sugar?"

"Here it is," said the Fairy, taking a lump from a golden sugar bowl.

"I want the sugar first, then I'll drink the bitter water."

"Do you promise?"

"Yes"

The Fairy gave him the sugar and Pinocchio, after chewing and swallowing it, said, smacking his lips:

"If only sugar were medicine! I should take it every day."

"Now keep your promise and drink these few drops of water. They'll be good for you."

Pinocchio took the glass in both hands and stuck his nose into it. He lifted it to his mouth and once more stuck his nose into it.

"It is too bitter, much too bitter! I can't drink it."

"How do you know, when you haven't even tasted it?"

"I can imagine it. I smell it. I want another lump of sugar, then I'll drink it." The Fairy, with all the patience of a good mother, gave him more sugar and again handed him the glass.

"I can't drink it like that," the Puppet said, making more wry faces.

"Why?"

"Because that feather pillow on my feet bothers me." The Fairy took away the pillow.

"It's no use. I can't drink it even now."

"What's the matter now?"

"I don't like the way that door looks. It's half open." The Fairy closed the door.

"I won't drink it, cried Pinocchio, bursting out crying. I won't drink this awful water. I won't, I won't! No, no, no!

My boy, you'll be sorry."

"I don't care."

"In a few hours the fever will take you far away to another world."

"I don't care."

"Aren't you afraid of death?"

"Not a bit. I'd rather die than drink that awful medicine."

At that moment the door of the room flew open and in came four rabbits as black as ink, carrying a small black coffin on their shoulders.

"What do you want from me?" asked Pinocchio.

"We have come for you." said the largest rabbit.

"For me?" but I'm not dead yet!

"No, not dead yet; but you will be in a few moments since you have refused to take the medicine which would have made you well."

"Oh, Fairy, dear Fairy," the Puppet cried out, "Give me that glass! Quick, please! I do not want to die! No, no, not yet ....!" And holding the glass with his two hands, he swallowed the medicine at one gulp.

"Well, said the four rabbits, "this time we have made the trip for nothing." And turning on their heels, they marched solemnly out of the room, carrying their little black coffin and muttering and grumbling among themselves.

Suddenly Pinocchio felt fine. With one leap he was out of bed and in his clothes. The Fairy, seeing him run and jump around the room, said to him:

"My medicine was good for you after all, wasn't it?"

"Yes indeed, it has given me new life."

"Why then, did I have to beg you so hard to make you drink it?"

"I'm a boy, you see, and all boys hate medicine more than they do sickness."

"What a shame! Boys ought to know, after all, that medicine, taken in time, can save them from much pain and even from death."

"Next time I won't have to be begged so hard, I'll remember those black rabbits with the black coffin on their shoulders and I'll take the glass and glug! — down it will go!"

"Come here now and tell me how it came about that you found yourself in the hands of the Assassins."

"It happened that I met a Fox and a Cat, who asked me, 'Do you want the five pieces to become two thousand?' And I said 'Yes' and they said, 'Come with us to the Field of Wonders.' And I said, 'Let's go.' Then they said, 'let us stop at the Inn of the Red Lobster for dinner and after midnight we'll set out again.' We ate and went to sleep. When I awoke they were gone and I started out in the darkness all alone. On the road I met two Assassins dressed in black coal sacks, who said to me, 'Your money or your life!' and I said, 'I haven't any money; for you see, I had put the money under my tongue. One of them tried to put his hand in my mouth and I bit it off and spat it out; but it wasn't a hand, it was a cat's paw. And they ran after me and I ran and ran, till at last they caught me and tied my neck with a rope and hanged me to a tree, saying, 'Tomorrow we'll come back for you and you'll be dead and your mouth will be open, and then we'll take the gold pieces that you have hidden under your tongue.'

"Where are the gold pieces now?" the Fairy asked.

"I lost them." answered Pinocchio, but he told a lie, for he had them in his pocket. As he spoke, his nose, long though it was, became at least two inches longer.

"And where did you lose them?"

"In the wood near by." At this second lie, his nose grew a few more inches.

"If you lost them in the near by wood," said the Fairy, "we'll find them, for everything that is lost there is always found."

"Ah, now I remember," replied the Puppet, becoming more and more confused. "I did not lose the gold pieces, but I swallowed them when I drank the medicine." At this third lie, his nose became so long that he could not even turn around. If he turned to the right, he knocked it against the bed or into the window panes; if he turned to the left, he struck the walls or the door; if he raised it a bit, he almost put the Fairy's eyes out. The Fairy sat looking at him and laughing.

"Why do you laugh?" the Puppet asked her, worried now at the sight of his growing nose.

"I am laughing at your lies."

"How do you know I am lying?"

"Lies, my boy, are known in a moment. There are two kinds — lies with short legs, and lies with long noses. Yours, just now, happen to have long noses."

XVIII

PINOCCHIO FINDS THE FOX AND THE CAT AGAIN, AND GOES WITH THEM TO SOW THE GOLD PIECES IN THE FIELD OF WONDERS.

Pinocchio, not knowing where to hide his shame, tried to escape from the room, but his nose had become so long that he could not get it out the door. He cried as if his heart would break and mourned for hours. No matter how he tried, it would not go through the door. The Fairy showed no pity, as she was trying to teach him a lesson so that he would stop telling lies. But when she saw him, pale with fright and with eyes half out of his head with terror, she began to feel sorry for him and clapped her hands together. A thousand woodpeckers flew in through the window and settled themselves on Pinocchio's nose. They pecked and pecked so hard at that enormous nose that, in a few moments, it was a normal size again.

"How good you are dear Fairy," said Pinocchio, drying his eyes, "and how much I love you!"

"I love you, too" answered the Fairy, "and if you wish to stay with me, you may be my little brother and I'll be your dear sister."

"I should like to stay — but what about my poor Father?"

"I have thought of everything. Your Father has been sent for and before night he will be here."

"Really?" cried Pinocchio joyfully. "Then, my good Fairy, I should like to go to meet him. I cannot wait to see my dear Father, who has suffered so much for my sake."

"Surely; go along, but be careful not to lose your way. Take the wood path and you will surely meet him."

Pinocchio set out, and as soon as he found himself in the wood, he ran like a hare. When he reached the giant oak tree he stopped, for he thought he heard a rustle in the brush. He was right. There stood the Fox and the Cat, the two travelling companions with whom he had eaten at the Inn of the Red Lobster.

"Here comes our dear Pinocchio!" cried the Fox, hugging and kissing him.

"How did you happen here?"

"How did you happen here?" repeated the Cat.

"It's a long story," said the Puppet. Let me tell it to you. The other night, when you left me at the Inn, I met the Assassins on the road — "

"The Assassins?" Oh, my poor friend! And what did they want?"

"They wanted my gold pieces."

"Rascals! said the Fox.

"The worst sort of rascals!" added the Cat.

"But I began to run," continued the Puppet, "and they ran after me, until they overtook me and hanged me to the limb of that oak." Pinocchio pointed to the giant oak near by.

"Could anything be worse?" said the Fox. "What an awful world to live in! Where shall we find a safe place for gentlemen like ourselves?"

Pinocchio noticed that the Cat carried his right paw in a sling.

"What happened to your paw?" he asked. The Cat tried to answer, but he became so terribly twisted in his speech that the Fox had to help him out.

"My friend is too modest to answer. I'll answer for him. About an hour ago, we met an old wolf on the road. He was half starved and begged for help. Having nothing to give him, what do you think my friend did out of the kindness of his heart? With his teeth, he bit off the paw of his front foot and threw it to that poor beast, so that he might have something to eat." As he spoke, the Fox wiped off a tear.

Pinocchio whispered in the Cat's ear:

"If all the cats were like you, how lucky the mice would be!"

"And what are you doing here?" the Fox asked the Puppet.

"I am waiting for my Father, who will be here at any moment now."

"And your gold pieces?"

"I still have them in my pocket, except one which I spent at the Inn of the Red Lobster."

"To think that those four gold pieces might become two thousand tomorrow. Why don't you listen to me? Why don't you sow them in the Field of Wonders?"

"Today it is impossible. I'll go with you some other time."

"Another day will be too late," said the Fox.

"Why?"

"because that field has been bought by a very rich man, and today is the last day that it will be open to the public."

"How far is this Field of Wonders?"

"Only two miles away. Will you come with us? We'll be there in half an hour. You can sow the money, and, after a few minutes, you will gather your two thousand coins and return home rich. Are you coming?"

Pinocchio hesitated before answered, for he remembered the good Fairy, old Geppetto, and the advice of the Talking Cricket. Then he ended by doing what all foolish boys do, when they have no heart and little brain. He shrugged his shoulders and said to the Fox and the Cat:

"Let us go! I am with you."

And they went.

They walked and walked for half a day at least and at last they came to the town called the City of Simple Simons. As soon as they entered the town, Pinocchio noticed that all the streets were filled with hairless dogs, yawning from hunger; with sheared sheep, trembling with cold; with combless chickens, begging for a grain of wheat; with large butterflies, unable to use their wings because they had sold all their lovely colours; with tail-less peacocks, ashamed to show themselves; and with bedraggled pheasants, scuttling away hurriedly, grieving for their bright feathers of gold and silver, lost to them forever.

Through this crowd of paupers and beggars, a beautiful coach passed now and again. In it sat either a Fox, a Hawk or a Vulture.

"Where is the Field of Wonders?" asked Pinocchio, growing tired of waiting.

"Be patient. It is only a few more steps away." They passed through the city and, just outside the walls, stepped into a lonely field, which looked more or less like any other field.

"Here we are, " said the Fox to the Puppet, "Dig a hole here and put the gold pieces in it.

The Puppet obeyed. He dug the hole, put the four gold pieces into it, and covered them very carefully. "Now," said the Fox, "go to the near by brook, bring back a pail of water, and sprinkle it over the spot." Pinocchio followed the directions closely, as he had no pail, he pulled off his shoe, filled it with water, and sprinkled the earth which covered the gold. Then he asked:

"Anything else?"

"Nothing else," answered the Fox. "Now we can go. Return here within twenty minutes and you will find the vine grown and the branches filled with gold pieces."

Pinocchio, beside himself with joy, thanked the Fox and the Cat many times and promised them each a beautiful gift. "We don't want any of your gifts," answered the two villains, "it is enough for us that we have helped you to become rich. For this makes us both very happy." They said good-bye to Pinocchio and wishing him good luck, went on their way.

XIX

PINOCCHIO IS ROBBED OF HIS GOLD PIECES AND, IN PUNISHMENT, IS SENTENCED TO FOUR MONTHS IN PRISON.

If the Puppet had been told to wait a day instead of twenty minutes, the time could not have seemed longer. He walked impatiently to and fro and finally turned toward the Field of Wonders. And as he walked with hurried steps his heart beat with an excited tic, tac, tic, tac, just as if it were a wall clock, and his busy brain kept thinking: "What if, instead of a thousand, I should find two thousand? Or perhaps five thousand, even one hundred thousand gold pieces? I'll build myself a beautiful palace, with a thousand stables filled with a thousand wooden horses to play with, a cellar overflowing with lemonade and ice cream soda, and a library of sweets and fruits, cakes and cookies.

Thus amusing himself with fancies, he came to the field. There he stopped to see if, by any chance, a vine filled with gold coins was in sight. But he saw nothing! He took a few steps forward, and still nothing! He went up to the place where he had dug the hole and buried the gold pieces. Again nothing! Pinocchio became very thoughtful and, forgetting good manners, he pulled a hand out of his pocket and scratched his head. As he did so, he heard a hearty burst of laughter close by. He turned sharply, and there just above him on the branch of a tree, sat a large Parrot, busily preening his feathers.
"What are you laughing at?" Pinocchio asked peevishly.
"I am laughing because, in preening my feathers, I tickled myself under the wings."
"The Puppet did not answer. He walked to the brook, filled his shoe with water, and once more sprinkled the ground which covered the gold pieces.

Another burst of laughter, even more impertinent than the first was heard.
"Well," cried the Puppet angrily this time, "may I know, Mr Parrot what amuses you?"
"I am laughing at those simpletons who believe everything they hear and allow themselves to be caught so easily in the traps set for them."
"Do you perhaps mean me?"
"I certainly do mean you, poor Pinocchio. You who are so silly as to believe that gold can be sown in a field just like beans or squash. I, too, believed that once. Today (but too late!) I have reached the conclusion that, in order to get money honestly, one must know how to earn it with a hand or brain."
"I don't know what you are talking about," said the Puppet, who was beginning to tremble with fear.
"I'll explain myself better," said the Parrot. "While you were in the city, the Fox and the Cat returned here in a great hurry. They took the four gold pieces which you had buried and ran away. You won't catch up with them now."

Pinocchio's mouth opened wide. He would not believe the Parrot's words and

began to dig away, furiously at the earth. He dug and he dug till the hole was as big as himself, but no money was there. Every gold piece was gone. In desperation he ran to the city and went straight to the courthouse to report the robbery to the magistrate.

The judge was a monkey, a large gorilla venerable with age. A flowing white beard covered his chest and he wore gold-rimmed spectacles from which the glasses had dropped out. The reason for wearing these, he said, was that his eyes had been weakened by the work of many years. Pinocchio standing before him, told his pitiful tale, word by word. He gave the names and the description of the robbers and begged for justice. The judge listened to him with great patience. A kind look shone in his eyes. He became very much interested in the story; he felt moved, and almost wept. When the Puppet had ended his tale the judge put out his hand and rang a bell. Two large mastiffs appeared, wearing police uni-The Magistrate, pointing to Pinocchio, said in a very solemn voice: "This poor simpleton has been robbed of four gold pieces. Take him, therefore, and throw him into prison."

The Puppet, on hearing the sentence passed upon him was stunned. He tried to protest, but the two officers clapped their paws over his mouth and hustled him away to jail. There he had to remain for five long, weary months. And if it had not been for a very lucky chance, he probably would have had to stay there longer. But it happened just then that the young Emperor, who ruled over the City of Simple Simons, had gained a great victory over his enemy, and in celebration had ordered illuminations, fireworks, shows of all kinds for his subjects, and, best of all, the opening of all prison doors.
"If the others go, I go too," said Pinocchio to the jailer.
"Not you," answered the jailer —" you are one of those —"
"I beg your pardon," interrupted Pinocchio, "I too, am a thief."
"In that case you also are free," said the jailer. Taking off his cap, he bowed low and opened the door of the prison, and Pinocchio ran out and away, with never a backward look.

FREED FROM PRISON, PINOCCHIO SETS OUT TO RETURN TO THE FAIRY; BUT ON THE WAY HE MEETS A SERPENT AND LATER IS CAUGHT IN A TRAP.

You can imagine how happy Pinocchio was to be free again. He fled from the city and set out on the road that would take him back to the house of the good Fairy. It had rained for many days, and the road was so muddy that, at times Pinocchio sank down almost to his knees, but he kept on bravely. Tormented by the wish to see his Father and his Fairy sister with blue hair, he raced like a greyhound, splashed with mud up to his cap.

"How unhappy I have been," he said to himself, but I certainly have been very stubborn and stupid, and so deserve my misfortunes. I always insist on having my own way, and won't listen to those who love me and have more brains that I. But from now on, I'll be different and I'll try to become obedient. I have found out, beyond any doubt that disobedience makes a boy unhappy. I wonder if Father is waiting for me. Will I find him at the Fairy's house? It has been so long since I have seen him. And will the Fairy ever forgive me for all I have done? Can there be a worse or more heartless boy than I am, I ran away from everyone who loved and cared for me."

Suddenly he stopped, frozen with fear. An immense Serpent lay stretched across the road - a serpent with bright green skin, fiery eyes which glowed and burned, and a pointed tail that smoked like a chimney. Pinocchio ran back wildly for half a mile, and settled himself on top of a heap of stones to wait for the Serpent to go on his way and leave the road clear. He waited an hour; two hours; three hours, but the Serpent was always there, and even from afar one could see the flash of his red eyes and the column of smoke which rose from his long pointed tail.

Pinocchio, trying to feel brave, walked up to him and said in a sweet, soothing voice: "I beg your pardon, Mr Serpent, would you be so kind as to step aside to let me pass," The Serpent never moved. Once more, in the same sweet voice, he spoke: "You must know, Mr Serpent, that I am going home where my Father is waiting for me. Would you mind if I passed?" He waited for some sign of an answer to his questions, but no answer came. On the contrary, the green Serpent, who had seemed until then wide awake and full of life, became suddenly very quiet and still. His eyes closed and his tail stopped smoking. "Is he dead, I wonder?" said Pinocchio. He started to step over the Serpent but he had just raised one leg when the Serpent shot up like a spring and the Puppet fell head over heels backward. He fell so awkwardly that his head stuck in the mud, and there he remained with his legs straight up in the air.

At the sight of the Puppet kicking and squirming the Serpent laughed so heartily and so long that he burst an artery and died on the spot. Pinocchio freed himself from his awkward position and once more began to run in order to reach the Fairy's house before dark. As he went, pangs of hunger grew so strong that, unable to withstand them, he jumped into a field to pick a few grapes that tempted him. No sooner had he reached the grapevine than — crack, a heavy steel trap gripped his legs, and he was unable to move.

The poor Puppet was caught in the trap set there by a farmer for some weasels which came regularly to steal his chickens.

XXI

PINOCCHIO IS TRAPPED BY A FARMER, WHO
USES HIM AS A WATCHDOG

Pinocchio, as you may well imagine, began to scream and weep and beg; but all was silent, no one passed by on the road, and no houses were to be seen. Night came on. Because of fright at finding himself alone in the darkness of the field, the Puppet felt quite faint. He saw a tiny glow worm flickering by, and called to her, saying:
"Dear little Glow worm, will you set me free?"
"Poor little fellow!" replied the Glow worm, stopping to look at him with pity.
"How were you caught in this trap?"
"I stepped into the lonely field to take a few grapes and ... "
"Are the grapes yours?"
"No."
"Who has taught you to take things that do not belong to you?"
"I was hungry."
"Hunger is no reason for taking something which belongs to another."
"That's true!" cried Pinocchio in tears. "I won't do it again."

Just then, the conversation was interrupted by approaching footsteps. It was the owner of the field, who was coming on tiptoes to see if, by chance, he had caught the weasels which had been eating his chickens. Great was his surprise when, on holding up his

47

lantern, he saw that, instead of a weasel, he had caught a puppet!

"Ah, you little thief!" said the Farmer in an angry voice. "Are you the one who steals my chickens!"

"No, no!" cried Pinocchio, sobbing bitterly. "I came here only to take a very few grapes."

"He who steals grapes may very easily steal chickens also. I'll give you a lesson that you'll remember for a long while." He opened the trap, grabbed the Puppet by the collar and carried him to the house as if he were a puppy.

When they reached the yard in front of the house, he flung him to the ground, put a foot on his neck, and said to him roughly: "It is late now and time for bed. Tomorrow we'll settle matters. In the meantime, since my watchdog died today, you may take his place and guard my hen house. No sooner said than done. He slipped Melampo's collar around Pinocchio's neck and tightened it so that it would not come off. A long iron chain was tied to the collar. The other end of the chain was nailed to the wall. "If tonight it should happen to rain," said the Farmer, you can sleep in that little doghouse near by. You will find plenty of straw for a soft bed. It has been Melampo's bed for three years, and it should be good enough for you." The Farmer went into the house, closed the door and barred it. Poor Pinocchio huddled close to the doghouse more dead than alive from cold, hunger and fright. Now and again he pulled and tugged at the collar which nearly choked him, and cried.

XXII

PINOCCHIO CATCHES THE THIEVES AND IS RELEASED BY THE FARMER AS A REWARD.

Boys seldom lose sleep over their worries, however unhappy and the Puppet was no exception to this rule. He slept on peacefully for a few hours when he was awakened by strange whisperings and stealthy sounds coming from the yard. He stuck his nose out of the doghouse and saw four slender, hairy animals. They were weasels, small animals very fond of both eggs and chickens. One of them left her companions and going to the door of the doghouse, said in a friendly voice:

"Good evening Melampo."

"My name is not Melampo," answered Pinocchio.

"Who are you then?"

" I am Pinocchio."

"What are you doing here?"

"I'm the watchdog."

"But where is Melampo? Where is the old dog who used to live in this house?"

"He died this morning."

"Died? Poor beast! He was so good! Still, judging by your face, I think you, too, are a good-natured dog."

"I beg your pardon, I am not a dog!"

"What are you then?"

"I am a Puppet."

"Are you taking the place of the watchdog?"

"I'm sorry to say that I am, I'm being punished!"

"Well, I shall make the same terms with you that we had with the dead Melampo. I am sure you will agree."

"And what are the terms?"

"This is our plan: We'll come once in a while, as in the past, to pay a visit to this henhouse, and that you will make believe you are sleeping and will not bark for the Farmer"

"Did Melampo really do that?" asked Pinocchio.

"Indeed he did, and because of that we were the best of friends. Sleep away peacefully, and remember that before we go we shall leave you a nice fat chicken all ready for your breakfast in the morning. Is that understood?"

"Only too well," answered Pinocchio, shaking his head in a threatening manner.

The four weasels went straight to the chicken coop which stood close to the doghouse. Digging busily with teeth and claws, they opened the little door and slipped in. But they were no sooner in than they heard the door close with a sharp bang.

Pinocchio had done this trick, and not satisfied with that, he dragged a heavy stone in front of it. That done, he started to bark as if he were a real dog. Bow, wow, wow! The Farmer heard the loud barks and jumped out of bed. Taking his gun, he leaped to the window and shouted:

"What's the matter."

"The thieves are here," answered Pinocchio, "in the chicken coop."

"I'm coming down," called the Farmer.

And, in fact, he was down in the yard in seconds and running toward the chicken coop. He opened the door, pulled out the weasels one by one, and after tying them in a bag, laughed happily and said "I've got them at last, my thanks to you boy, that was very good work — and to think that my faithful Melampo never saw them in all these years!"

The Puppet could have told all he knew about the shameful contract between the dog and the weasels, but thinking of the dead dog, he said to himself: "Melampo is dead. What is the use of accusing him? The dead cannot defend themselves. The best thing to do is to leave them in peace!"

"Were you awake or asleep when they came?" asked the Farmer.

"I was asleep," answered Pinocchio, "they awakened me with their whisperings. One of them even came to the door of the doghouse and said to me: 'If you promise not to bark, we will make you a present of one of the chickens for your breakfast.' They had the audacity to make such a proposition to me! I may be a wicked Puppet, full of faults, but I have never yet taken a bribe."

"Fine boy! cried the Farmer, slapping him on the shoulder in a friendly way. You ought to be proud of yourself. And to show you what I think of you, you are free from this instant! and shall have a good breakfast!" And he slipped the dog collar from Pinocchio's neck.

XXIII

PINOCCHIO CRIES WHEN HE LEARNS THAT THE LOVELY MAIDEN WITH AZURE HAIR IS DEAD. HE MEETS A PIGEON, WHO CARRIES HIM TO THE SEA SHORE. HE THROWS HIM-SELF INTO THE SEA TO HELP HIS FATHER.

When Pinocchio left the Farmer, freed of the shameful weight of the dog collar, he started to run across the fields and meadows, and never stopped till he came to the main road that was to take him to the Fairy's house. When he reached it, he looked into the valley far below him and there he saw the wood where unluckily he had met the Fox and the Cat, and the tall oak tree where he had been hanged; but though he searched far and near, he could not see the house where the Fairy with the Azure Hair lived.

He became terribly frightened and, running as fast as he could he finally came to the spot where it had once stood. The little house was no longer there. In its place lay a small marble slab, which bore this sad inscription:

HERE LIES
THE LOVELY FAIRY WITH AZURE HAIR
WHO DIED OF GRIEF
WHEN
ABANDONED
BY
HER LITTLE BROTHER PINOCCHIO

The poor Puppet was heartbroken when he read these words. He fell to the ground and, covering the cold marble with kisses, burst into bitter tears. He cried all night, and dawn found him still there, though the tears had tried and only hard, dry sobs shook his wooden frame. As he sobbed he said to himself: "Oh my Fairy, my dear, dear Fairy, why did you die?" Why did not I die, who am so bad, instead of you. And my Father — where can he be? Please, dear Fairy, tell me where he is and I shall never, never leave him again! You are not really dead, are you? If you love me, you will come back, alive as before. I'm so lonely. What will I do alone in the world? Now that you are dead and my Father is lost, where shall I eat? Where shall I sleep? Who will make my new clothes? Oh, I want to die!"

Poor Pinocchio! He even tried to tear his hair, but as it was only painted on his wooden head, he could not even pull it. Just then a large Pigeon flew far above him. Seeing the Puppet, it cried to him:
"Tell me, little boy, what are you doing there?"

"Can't you see? I'm crying," cried Pinocchio, lifting his head toward the voice and rubbing his eyes with his sleeve.

"Tell me," asked the Pigeon, "do you by chance know of a Puppet, Pinocchio by name?"

"Pinocchio! Did you say Pinocchio?" replied the Puppet, jumping to his feet.

"Why, I am Pinocchio!"

At his answer the Pigeon flew swiftly down to the earth.

"Then you knew Geppetto also?"

"He's my Father, my poor dear Father! Has he, perhaps, spoken to you of me? Will you take me to him? Is he still alive? Answer me, please! Is he still alive?"

"I left him three days ago on the shore of a large sea."

"What was he doing?"

"He was building a little boat with which to cross the ocean. For the last four months that poor man has been wandering around Europe, looking for you. Not having found you yet, he has made up his mind to look for you in the New World, far across the sea."

"How far is it from here to the shore?" asked Pinocchio anxiously.

"More than fifty miles."

"Fifty miles? Oh, dear Pigeon, how I wish I had your wings!"

"If you want to come I'll take you with me."

"How?"

"Astride my back. Are you very heavy?"

"Heavy?" Not at all. I'm only a featherweight."

"Very well." Saying nothing more, Pinocchio jumped on the Pigeon's back and, they were soon flying towards the ocean. The puppet holding on very tight to his feathery steed, as he looked down at the world below, growing smaller as they flew ever higher, making him feel giddy and fearful of falling off.

They flew all day. Toward evening the Pigeon said:

"I'm very thirsty!"

"And I'm very hungry! said Pinocchio. "Let us stop a few minutes at that dovecote down there. Then we can go on and be at the seashore in the morning."

They went into the empty dovecote and there they found nothing but a bowl of water and a small basket filled with chick-peas. The Puppet had always hated chick-peas. According to him they had always made him sick; but that night he ate them with relish. As he finished them, he turned to the Pigeon saying "I never should have thought that chick-peas could be so good."

"Well, answered the Pigeon, hunger is always the best sauce!"

After resting a few minutes longer, they set out again. The next morning they were at the seashore. Pinocchio jumped off the Pigeon's back, and the bird, not wanting any thanks for a kind deed, flew away swiftly and disappeared.

The shore was full of people, crying and pointing out over the sea.

"What has happened?" Pinocchio asked a little old woman.

"A poor old man lost his only son some time ago and today he finished building a tiny boat for himself in order to go in search for him across the ocean. The water is very rough and we're afraid he will be drowned..."

"Where is the little boat?"

"There. Straight down there," answered the little old woman, pointing to a tiny shadow, no

larger than a nutshell, floating on the sea. Pinocchio looked for a few moments and then gave a sharp cry: "It's my Father! It's my Father!"

Meanwhile the little boat, tossed about by the angry waters, appeared and disappeared in the waves. And Pinocchio, standing on a high rock, tired out with searching, waved to him with hand and cap. It looked as if Geppetto, though far away from the shore, recognized his son, for he took off his cap and waved also. He seemed to be trying to make everyone understand that he would come back if he were able, but the sea was so heavy that he could do nothing with his oars. Suddenly a huge wave came and the boat disappeared. They waited and waited for it, but it was gone. "Poor man!" said the fisher folk, whispering a prayer as they turned to go home. Just then a desperate cry was heard. Turning around, the fisherpeople saw Pinocchio dive into the sea and heard him cry out: "I'll save him! I'll save my Father!"

The Puppet, being made of wood, floated easily along and swam like a fish in the rough water. Now and again he disappeared only to reappear once more, and was soon far away from land. He was finally completely lost to view.

XXIV

PINOCCHIO REACHES THE ISLAND OF THE BUSY BEES AND FINDS THE FAIRY ONCE MORE.

Pinocchio swam all night long — and what a horrible night it was! It poured rain, it hailed, it thundered, and the lightning was so bright that it turned night into day. At dawn, he saw, not far away from him, a long stretch of sand. It was an island. Pinocchio tried to reach it but could not. The waves tossed him about as if he were a twig or a piece of straw. Then luckily for him, a tremendous wave tossed him to the very spot where he wanted to be. The blow from the wave was so strong that, as he fell to the ground, his joints creaked and almost broke, but nothing daunted, he jumped to his feet and cried: "I reached the Island, once more I have escaped danger with my life!"

Little by little the sky cleared. The sun came out and the sea became as calm as a lake. The Puppet took off his clothes and laid them on the sand to dry. He looked over the waters to see whether he might catch sight of a boat with a little man in it. He searched the horizon but saw nothing except sea and sky, and far away a few sails. "If only I knew the name of this island!" he said to himself." But whom shall I ask? The idea of finding himself in so lonesome a spot made him sad and he was about to cry, but just then he saw a big fish swimming nearby, with his head far out of the water. Not knowing what to call him, the Puppet called out to him:

"Hey there, Mr Fish, may I have a word with you?"

"As many words as you want," answered the fish, who was a very polite Dolphin.

"Will you please tell me if, on this island, there are places where one may eat without necessarily being eaten?"

"Surely, there are," answered the Dolphin. "In fact you'll find one not far from this spot."

"And how shall I get there?"

"Take that path on your left and follow your nose. You can't go wrong."

"Tell me another thing. You who travel day and night through the sea. Did you perhaps see a little boat with my Father in it?"

"In the storm of last night," answered the Dolphin, "I fear the little boat must have been swamped." and your Father may have been swallowed by the Terrible Shark, which, for the last few days, has been bringing terror to these waters."

"Is this Shark very big?" asked Pinocchio, who was beginning to tremble with fright.

"Is he big?" replied the Dolphin. "Just to give you an idea of his size, let me tell you that he is larger than a five story building and that he has a mouth so big and so deep that a whole train and engine could easily get into it."

"Good heavens!" cried the Puppet, scared to death and dressing himself as fast as he could, he turned to the Dolphin and said: "Farewell Mr Fish, and many thanks for your kindness." Then he took the path at so swift a gait that he seemed to fly, and at every small sound he heard, he turned in fear to see whether the Terrible Shark, five stories high and with a train in his mouth, was following him.

After half an hour he arrived at the main town of a small country called the Land of Busy Bees. The streets were filled with people running to and fro about their tasks.Everyone worked, everyone had something to do. Even if one were to search the town, not one idle man or a tramp could have been found. "I understand," said Pinocchio, wearily looking around, "this is no place for me! I was not born for work." But in the meantime, he began to feel hungry. What was to be done? There were only two means left to him to get a bite to eat — to work or to beg. He was ashamed to beg, because his Father had always told him that only the truly poor of this world, those who because of illness or age, were unable to earn their living, should beg. All others should work, and if they didn't, and went hungry, so much the worse for them.

Just then a man passed by, worn out and wet with perspiration, pulling with difficulty two heavy carts filled with coal. Pinocchio looked at him and, judging him by his looks to be a kind man, said to him with eyes downcast in shame:

"Will you be so good as to give me a penny, for I am faint with hunger?"

"Not only one penny," answered the coal man, "I'll give you four if you will help me pull these two carts."

The Puppet was very much offended.

"I wish you to know that I never have been a donkey, nor have I ever pulled a cart."
"Then my boy, answered the coalman, if you are really faint with hunger, eat two slices of your pride; and I hope they don't give you indigestion."

A few minutes later, a bricklayer passed by, carrying a pail full of plaster on his shoulder.
"Good man, will you be kind enough to give a penny to a poor boy who is yawning from hunger?"
"Gladly, answered the bricklayer, "Come with me and carry some plaster, and instead of one penny, I'll give you five."
"But the plaster is heavy," answered Pinocchio, "and the work too hard for me."
"If the work is too hard for you, my boy, enjoy your yawns and may they bring you luck." In less than half an hour, at least twenty people passed and Pinocchio begged of each one, but they all answered: Aren't you ashamed? Instead of being a beggar in the streets, why don't you look for work and earn your own bread?" Finally a little woman went by, carrying two water jugs. "Good Woman, will you allow me to have a drink from one of your jugs?" asked Pinocchio, who was burning up with thirst. "With pleasure, my lad!" she answered, setting the two jugs and a cup on the ground before him. When Pinocchio had had his fill, he grumbled as he wiped his mouth. "My thirst is gone. If I could only get rid of my hunger now."

On hearing these words, the good little woman immediately said: "If you help

55

me to carry these jugs home, I'll give you a big slice of bread and butter." Pinocchio looked at the jug and said neither yes nor no. "And with the bread, I'll give you a nice dish of cauliflower with sauce on it." Pinocchio gave the jug another look and said nothing. "And after the cauliflower, some cake and sweets." At this last bribery, Pinocchio could no longer resist and said firmly: "Very well, I'll take the jug home for you."

The jug was very heavy, and the Puppet, not being strong enough to carry it with his hands, had to put it on his head. When they arrived home, the little woman sat Pinocchio down at a small table and placed before him the bread, the cauliflower and the cake and sweets Pinocchio did not eat; he just devoured the food. His stomach seemed a bottomless pit.

His hunger finally appeased, he raised his head to thank his kind benefactress. But he had not looked at her long when he gave a cry of surprise and sat there with his eyes open, his fork in the air, and his mouth filled with bread and cauliflower. "Why all this surprise?" asked the good woman, laughing. "Because – " answered Pinocchio, stammering and stuttering, "because – you look like – you remind me of – yes, yes, the same voice, the same eyes, the same hair – yes, yes, you also have the same azure hair she had – Oh, my little Fairy, my dear Fairy! Tell me that it is you! Don't make me cry any longer! If you only knew! I have cried so much, I have suffered so .....!" And Pinocchio threw himself on the floor and clasped the knees of the mysterious little woman.

XXV

PINOCCHIO PROMISES THE FAIRY TO BE GOOD AND TO STUDY, AS HE IS GROWING TIRED OF BEING A PUPPET AND WISHES TO BECOME A REAL BOY.

Pinocchio cried so much the little woman thought he would melt away, so she finally admitted that she was the Fairy with Azure Hair.
"You naughty Puppet! How did you know it was I?' she asked, laughing.
"My love for you told me who you were."
"Do you remember? You left me when I was a young girl and now you find me a grown woman. I am so old, I could almost be your mother!"
"I am very glad of that, for then I can call you Mother instead of Sister. For a long time I have wanted a mother, just like other boys. But how did you grow so quickly?"
"That's a secret!"
"Tell it to me. I also want to grow a little. Look at me! I have never grown any higher than I was when my dear Father found me in the wooden log."
"But you can't grow," answered the Fairy.
"Why not?"
"Because Puppets never grow. They are born Puppets, they live and die Puppets.
"Oh, I'm tired of always being a Puppet!" cried Pinocchio disgustedly. "It's about time for me to grow into a man as everyone else does."
"And you will if you deserve it."
"Really? What can I do to deserve it?"

"It's a very simple matter. Just try to act like a well-behaved child."

"Don't you think I do?"

"Far from it! Good boys are obedient, and you, on the contrary ....."

"And I never obey."

"Good boys love study and work, but you ....."

"I am a lazy fellow and do not think I should work."

"Good boys always tell the truth."

"And I tell lies."

"Good boys go gladly to school."

"And I get sick if I go to school. But from now on I'll be different."

"Do you promise?"

"I promise. I want to be a good boy and a comfort to my Father. Where is my poor father?"

"I do not know."

"Will I ever be lucky enough to find him again?"

"I think so. Indeed, I am sure of it."

"At this answer, Pinocchio's happiness was very great. He grasped the Fairy's hands and kissed them. Then, lifting his face, he looked at her movingly and asked:

"Tell me, little Mother, it isn't true that you are dead, is it?"

"It doesn't seem so," answered the Fairy, smiling.

"If you only knew how I suffered and how I wept when I read 'Here lies ..... "

"I know it, and for that I have forgiven you. The depth of your sorrow made me see that you have a kind heart. This is the reason why I have come so far to look for you. From now on, I'll be your own little Mother.

"Oh! How lovely!" cried Pinocchio, jumping with joy.

"You will obey me always and do as I wish?"

"Gladly, more than gladly!"

"Beginning tomorrow," said the Fairy, "You'll go to school every day. Then you will choose the trade you like best." Pinocchio became more serious.

"What are you mumbling to yourself?" asked the Fairy.

"I was just saying," whined the Puppet in a whisper, "that it seems too late for me to go to school now."

"No, indeed. Remember it is never too late to learn."

"But I don't want either a trade or a profession."

"Why?"

"Because I don't like work."

"My dear boy," said the Fairy, "people who speak as you do usually end their days either in prison or in a hospital. A man, whether rich or poor, should do something in this world. No one can find happiness without work. Woe betide the lazy fellow. Laziness is a serious illness and one must cure it, even from early childhood. Otherwise it can destroy your life."

These words touched Pinocchio's heart. He lifted his eyes to his Fairy and said seriously:

"I'll work: I'll study: I'll do all you tell me. After all, the life of a Puppet has grown very tiresome to me and I want to become a boy, no matter how hard it may be. You promise that, do you not?"

"Yes, I promise, and now it is up to you."

XXVI

PINOCCHIO GOES TO THE SEA SHORE WITH HIS FRIENDS TO SEE THE TERRIBLE SHARK.

In the morning, bright and early, Pinocchio started for school. Imagine what the boys said when they saw a Puppet enter the class room! Everyone played tricks on him. One pulled his hat off, another tugged at his coat, a third tried to paint a mustache under his nose. One even attempted to tie strings to his feet and hands to make him dance.

For a while Pinocchio was very calm and quiet. Finally, however he lost all patience and, turning to his tormentors, he said threateningly:

"Careful, boys, I haven't come here to be made fun of. I'll respect you and I want you to respect me."

"Hurrah for Dr Know-all! You speak like a printed book!" howled the boys, laughing loudly. One of them, more impudent than the rest, put out his hand to pull the Puppet's nose. But he was not quick enough, for Pinocchio stretched his leg under the table and kicked him hard on the shin.

"Oh, what hard feet!" cried the boy, rubbing the spot where he had been kicked.

"And what elbows! They are even harder than the feet!" shouted another, who, because of some other trick, had received a blow in the stomach. With that kick and blow, Pinocchio gained everybody's favour. Everyone admired him, and danced attendance on him.

As the days passed into weeks, even the teacher praised him, for he saw him attentive, and hard working, always the first to arrive in the morning, and the last to leave when school was over. Pinocchio's only fault was that he had too many friends. Among these were many well-known rascals, who cared not a jot for study or for success. The teacher warned him each day, and even the good Fairy repeated to him many times.

"Take care, Pinocchio! Those bad companions will sooner or later make you lose your love for study. Some day they will lead you astray."

"There's no such danger," answered the Puppet, pointing to his forehead, as if to say: "I am too wise!"

So it happened that one day, as he was walking to school, he met some boys who ran up to him and said:

"Have you heard the news?"

"No!"

"A Shark as big as a mountain has been seen near the shore."

"Really? I wonder if it could be the same one I heard of when my Father was drowned?"

"We are going to the shore to see it. Are you coming?"

"No, I must go to school."

"What do you care about school?" You can go there tomorrow. With a lesson more or less, we are always the same donkeys."

"And what will the teacher say?"

"Let him talk. He is paid to grumble all day long."

"And my Mother?"

"Mothers don't know anything," answered those bad boys.

"Well, said Pinocchio for reasons of my own, I too want to see that Shark, but I'll go to school first."

"Poor Fool!" cried one of the boys, "do you think that a fish of that size will stand there waiting for you?" He will go soon, and none of us will see him again."

"How long does it take to get from here to the shore?"

"One hour there and back."

"Very well, then, let's see who gets there first!" Cried Pinocchio, setting off at a great pace.

At the signal, the little troop, with books under their arms, dashed across the fields. Now and again Pinocchio looked back and laughed, seeing his followers panting and hot, trying hard to keep up with him.

If he had only known then the dreadful things that were to happen to him because of his disobedience!

XXVII

THE GREAT BATTLE BETWEEN
PINOCCHIO AND HIS PLAYMATES.
ONE IS WOUNDED. PINOCCHIO IS
ARRESTED.

Pinocchio soon reached the shore. He glanced about him, but there was no sign of a Shark. The sea was smooth as glass.

"Hey there, boys! Where's the Shark?" he asked, turning to his playmates.

"He may have gone for his breakfast," said one of them laughing.

"Or, perhaps he went to bed for a little nap," said another, laughing also.

From the foolish answers and the laughter which followed them, Pinocchio understood that the boys had played a trick on him, and he said angrily,

"What's the joke?"

"Oh, the joke's on you!" cried his tormentors, laughing more heartily than ever, "we have made you stay out of school to come with us. Aren't you ashamed of being such a goody, goody, and studying so hard? You never have any fun."

"What is it to you if I do study?"

"Don't you see? If you study and we don't, we get into trouble with the teachers. After all, it's only fair to look out for ourselves."

"What do you expect me to do?"

"Just to hate school and books and teachers, as we all do.

"And if I go on studying, what will you do then?"

"You'll pay for it! We'll get even with you..."

"Really, you amuse me," answered the Puppet, shaking his head.

"Hey, Pinocchio," cried the tallest of them all, "that's enough, we are tired of hearing you bragging about yourself! You may not be afraid of us, but remember we are not afraid of you either! You are alone, you know, and there are seven of us!"

"Like the Seven Sins." said Pinocchio, still laughing.

"Did you hear that? He has insulted us all. He has called us sins."

"Pinocchio, apologize for that, or look out!"

Cuck—oo!" said the Puppet, mocking them with his thumb to his nose.

"You'll be sorry!"

"Cuck—oo!"

"You'll go home with a broken nose!"

"Cuck—oo!"

"Very well, then! Take that, and keep it for your supper," called out the boldest of the gang." And with the words, he gave Pinocchio a terrible blow on the head. Pinocchio answered with another blow, and that was the signal for the beginning of the fray. In a few moments the fight raged hot and heavy. Pinocchio, although alone, defended himself bravely. With those two wooden feet, he worked so fast that his opponents kept at a respectful distance. Wherever they landed, they left their painful mark.

Enraged at not being able to fight the Puppet at close quarters, they started to throw all kinds of books at him. Readers, geographies, histories, grammars flew in all directions. But Pinocchio was keen of eye and swift of movement, and the books only passed over his head, landed in the sea and disappeared.

The battle became more and more furious. At the noise, a large crab crawled slowly out of the water and, with a voice that sounded like a trombone suffering from a cold, he

cried out: "Stop fighting you rascals! These battles between boys rarely end well, and ill will come of it. You'll see!" He might as well have spoken to the wind. Instead of listening to his good advice, Pinocchio turned to him and said roughly: "Quiet, ugly crab. It would be better for you to chew a few cough drops to get rid of that cold you have, than give other people advice."

Meanwhile the boys, having used up all their books, looked around for new ammunition. Seeing Pinocchio's books lying nearby, they took them. One of these books was his favourite, a large, heavily bound geography text, and it promised to be an excellent missile. One of the boys took hold of it and threw it with all his strength at Pinocchio's head. But instead of hitting the Puppet, the book struck one of the other boys, who, pale as a ghost, cried out "Help! I'm dying!" and fell senseless to the ground.

At the sight of that pale little body, the boys were so frightened that they turned and ran. In a few moments all had disappeared. All except Pinocchio. Although scared to death at what had happened, he ran to the sea and soaked his handkerchief in the cool water and with it bathed the head of his poor little school mate. Sobbing bitterly, he called to him saying: "Eugene! Poor Eugene! Open your eyes! Why don't you answer? I was not the one who hit you, you know. Believe me, I didn't do it. Open your eyes, Eugene! If you don't open your eyes, I'll die too! How can I ever go home now? How shall I ever look at my little Mother again? Where shall I go? Where shall I hide? Oh, how much better it would have been if only I had gone to school! Why did I listen to those boys? And to think that the teacher told me — and my Mother too — 'Beware of bad company!' That's what they said. But I'm stubborn and proud. I listen, but always do as I wish, and then I pay for it. What will become of me. Oh, what will become of me?"

Pinocchio went on crying and moaning and beating his head. Again and again he called to his little friend, who still lay as he fallen, pale and still. Suddenly he heard heavy steps approaching. He looked up and saw two policemen near him.

"What are you doing lying here?" they asked Pinocchio.

"I am trying to help my schoolfellow."

"Has he fainted?"

"I should say so," said one of the officers bending to look at Eugene. "This boy has been wounded on the temple. Who has hurt him"

"Not I," stammered the Puppet, who had hardly a breath left in his whole body.

"If it wasn't you, who was it then?"

"Not I," repeated Pinocchio.

"And how was he wounded?"

"With this book," said the Puppet, picking up the heavy book to show it to the officer.

"And whose book is this?"

"Mine."

"Enough. Not another word! Get up quickly and come along with us."

"But I ....."

"Come with us!"

"But I am innocent."

"Come with us!"

62

Before starting out the officers called out to several fishermen passing by in a boat and said to them "Take care of this little fellow who has been hurt. Take him home and bind his wound. Tomorrow we'll come for him." They then took hold of Pinocchio and, putting him between them, said to him in a rough voice: "March! and quickly, or it will be the worse for you!"

They did not have to repeat the words. The Puppet walked swiftly along the road to the village. But the poor fellow hardly knew what he was doing. He felt ill. His eyes saw everything double, his legs trembled, his tongue was dry, and, try as he might, he could not utter a single word. Yet, in spite of this numbness of feeling, he suffered keenly at the thought of passing under the window of his good Fairy's house. What would she say on seeing him between two policemen? They had just reached the village, when a sudden gust of wind blew off Pinocchio's cap and it went sailing down the street.
"Would you allow me," the Puppet asked the policemen, "to run and get my cap?"
"Very well, but hurry."

The Puppet went, picked up his cap — but instead of putting it on his head, he stuck it between his teeth and raced for the sea. He went like a bullet out of a gun. The police officers, judging that it would be difficult to catch him, sent a large mastiff after him. Pinocchio ran fast and the dog ran faster.

At so much noise, the people hung out of the windows or gathered in the street, anxious to see the end of the contest. But they were disappointed, for the dog and Pinocchio raised so much dust on the road that, after a few moments it was impossible to see them.

XXVIII

PINOCCHIO IS ALMOST FRIED IN
A PAN LIKE A FISH.

During that wild chase, Pinocchio lived through a terrible moment when he almost gave himself up as lost. This was when Alidoro (that was the mastiff's name), came so near that he was on the very point of reaching him. The Puppet heard, close behind him the laboured breathing of the dreadful beast so close on his trail, and now and then even felt his hot breath blow over him. Luckily, by this time he was very near the shore, and the sea only a few short steps away.

As he set foot on the beach, Pinocchio gave a great leap out into the water. Alidoro tried to stop, but as he was running very fast, he was unable to, and he, too, landed far out in the sea. Strange though it may seem, the dog could not swim. He beat the water with his paws to keep his nose up, but the harder he tried, the deeper he sank. As he stuck his head out once more, the poor fellow's eyes were bulging and he barked out wildly:
"I drown! I drown! Help, Pinocchio! Save me from death!"
At those cries of suffering, the Puppet, who had a kind heart, was moved to pity. He turned toward the struggling animal and said to him:
"If I help you, will you promise not to run after me again?"
"I promise! I promise! Only hurry, for I am drowning now!"
Pinocchio hesitated still, then, remembering how his Father had often told him that a kind

deed is never lost, he swam to Alidoro and, catching hold of his tail, dragged him to the shore. The poor dog was so weak he could not stand, and had swallowed much salt water. However, Pinocchio, not wishing to trust him too much, threw himself once again into the sea, and as he swam away, called out:

"Good-bye Alidoro, good luck."

"Good-bye, little Pinocchio," answered the dog. "A thousand thanks for saving me. You did me a good turn, and I shall not forget you."

Pinocchio swam on, close to shore. At last he thought he had reached a safe place. He saw the opening of a cave out of which rose a spiral of smoke. He said to himself "There must be a fire in that cave and I'll be able to dry my clothes and warm myself." He swam to the rocks, but as he started to climb, he felt something under him lifting him up higher and higher. He tried to escape, but was too late. To his great surprise he found himself in a large net, amid a crowd of fish of all kinds and sizes who were struggling desperately to free themselves. At the same time he saw a Fisherman come out of the cave, a Fisherman so ugly that Pinocchio thought he was a sea monster. In place of hair, his head was covered by a thick bush of green grass. Green was the skin of his body, green were his eyes, and the long, long beard that reached down to his feet. He looked like a giant lizard with legs and arms.

When the Fisherman pulled the net out of the sea, he cried out happily, "Splenddid catch! Today I'll have a good meal of fish."

"Thank heaven I'm not a fish!" said Pinocchio to himself, trying with these words to find a little courage. The Fiserman took the net and the fish to the cave; a dark, gloomy, smoky place. In the middle was a pan full of oil, sizzling over a smoky fire, sending out a breathtaking stench of oil.

"Now, let's see what kind of fish we have caught today," said the Green Fisherman. He put a hand as big as a spade into the net and pulled out a handful of mullet. "Fine mullet these!" he said, after looking at them and smelling them with pleasure. After that, he threw them into a large empty tub. Many times he repeated this performance. As he pulled each fish out of the net, his mouth watered with the thought of the good dinner coming, and he said: "Fine fish these bass!" "Delicious flounders, these!" "What splendid crabs!" "And these dear little anchovies, with their heads still on!" As you can imagine, the bass, the flounders, the white fish, and even the little anchovies all went together into the tub to keep the mullet company.

The last to come out of the net was Pinocchio. As soon as the Fisherman pulled his out, his green eyes opened wide with surprise, and he cried out "What kind of fish is this? I don't recall ever eating anything like it." He looked at the Puppet closely, and after turning him over and over, he said at last: " I know, he must be a crab!"

"What nonsense," Pinocchio cried out resentfully. "Crab indeed! I am no such thing — I am a Puppet, I'll have you know."

"Well, said the Fisherman, I must admit that a Puppet fish is for me an entirely new kind of fish. So much the better, I'll eat you with greater relish."

"Eat me? But can't you understand that I'm not a fish? Can't you hear that I speak and think as you do?"

"It's true," answered the Fisherman; "but since I see that you are a fish, well able to talk and think as I do, I'll treat you with all due respect."

"And that is .... ?"

"As a sign of my particular esteem, I'll leave to you the choice of the manner in which you

are to be cooked. Do you wish to be fried in a pan, or do you prefer to be cooked with tomato sauce?"

"To tell you the truth," replied Pinocchio, if I can choose, I should much rather go free so I may return home!"

"Certainly not. Do you think I want to lose the opportunity to taste such a rare fish? Leave it to me. I'll fry you in the pan with the others. I know you'll like it. It's always a comfort to find oneself in good company."

The unlucky Puppet, hearing this, began to cry and wail and beg. With tears streaming down his cheeks, he thought "How much better it would have been for me to go to school!" And as he struggled and squirmed like an eel to escape, the Green Fisherman took a stout cord, tied him hand and foot, and threw him into the bottom of the tub with the others. Then he pulled a wooden bowl full of flour out of a cupboard and started to roll the fish in it, one by one. When they were white with it, he threw them into the pan. The first to dance in the hot oil were the mullet, the bass followed, then the whitefish, the flounders and the anchovies. Pinocchio's turn came last. Seeing himself so near to death (and such a horrible death!) he began to tremble so with fright that he had no voice left with which to beg for his life. The poor boy beseeched only with his eyes. But the Green Fisherman, not even noticing that it was he, turned him over and over in the flour until he looked like a Puppet made of chalk.

XXIX

PINOCCHIO RETURNS TO THE FAIRY'S HOUSE AND SHE PROMISES HIM THAT THE FOLLOWING DAY HE WILL CEASE TO BE A PUPPET AND BECOME A BOY, AND A WONDERFUL PARTY IS PLANNED TO CELEBRATE THAT GREAT EVENT.

Mindful of what the Fisherman had said, Pinocchio felt that all hope of being saved had gone. He closed his eyes and waited for the final moment. Suddenly a large dog, attracted by the smell of cooking fish, came running into the cave. "Get out!" cried the Fisherman threateningly and still holding onto the Puppet, who was all covered with flour. But the Dog was very hungry, and whining and wagging his tail, he tried to say:
"Give me a bite of the fish and I'll go in peace."

"Get out, I say!" repeated the Fisherman, and he drew back to give the Dog a kick. Then the Dog, who was really hungry, turned in a rage toward the Fisherman, and bared his great fangs. And at that moment, a pitiful little voice was heard saying: "Save me, Alidoro; if you don't, I fry!" The Dog immediately recognized Pinocchio's voice. Great was his surprise to find that the voice came from the little flour-covered bundle that the Fisherman held in his hand.

With one great leap, he grasped that bundle in his mouth and, holding it lightly between his teeth, ran through the door and disappeared like a flash! The Fisherman, angry at seeing his meal snatched from under his nose, ran after the mastiff, but a bad fit of coughing made him stop and turn back. Meanwhile Alidoro, as soon as he had found the road which led to the village, stopped and dropped Pinocchio softly onto the ground.
"How can I thank you!" said the Puppet.

"It is not necessary," answered the Dog. "You saved me once, and one good deed deserves another, we are all in this world to help one another."

"But how did you get into that cave?"

"I was lying here on the sand more dead than alive, when an appetizing smell of fried fish came to me. That made me hungry and I followed it. I just arrived in time!"

"Don't speak about it," wailed Pinocchio, still trembling with fright. If you had come a moment later, I'd be fried, eaten and digested by this time - I shudder at the very thought of it."

Alidoro laughingly held out his paw to the Puppet, who shook it heartily, feeling that now he and the mastiff were very good friends indeed. Then they bid each other good-bye and the Dog went home.

Pinocchio walked toward a little hut nearby, where an old man sat at the door sunning himself, and asked:

"Tell me, good Sir, have you heard anything of a poor boy with a wounded head, whose name was Eugene?"

"The boy was brought to this hut and now .... "

"Now he is dead?" Pinocchio interrupted sorrowfully.

"No, he is alive and has already gone home."

"Really and truly?" cried the joyful Puppet. "Then the wound was not serious?"

"No, but it might have been — he might even have been killed. A very large book was thrown at his head."

"And who threw it?"

"A schoolmate of his, a certain Pinocchio."

"And who is this Pinocchio?" asked the Puppet, pretending to know nothing.

"They say he is a trouble-maker and a good-for-nothing.

"That's not true." said the Puppet.

"Do you know this Pinocchio?"

"I know of him," answered the Puppet.

"And what do you think of him?" asked the old man.

"I think he's a very good boy, fond of study, obedient, kind to his Father...."

As he was telling all these lies about himself, Pinocchio touched his nose and found it twice as long as it should be. Very frightened he cried out:

"Don't listen to me, all the wonderful things I have said are not true at all. I know Pinocchio well and he is indeed a bad fellow, lazy and disobedient, who instead of going to school, ran away with his playmates to have a good time." At this speech, his nose returned to its normal size.

"Why are you so pale?" the old man asked suddenly. "And what have you done with your coat, hat and trousers?"

"I met thieves and they robbed me. Tell me, have you not, perhaps a little suit to give me so that I may go home?"

"My boy, as for clothes, I have only a bag in which I keep hops. If you want it, take it. There it is." Pinocchio took the bag, and after cutting a big hole at the top and two at the sides, he slipped into it as if it were a shirt. Lightly clad as he was, he thanked the old man, and started out toward the village.

Along the way he felt very uneasy. In fact he was so unhappy that he went taking two steps forward and one back, and as he went he said to himself: "How shall I ever face my good little Fairy? What will she say when she sees me? Will she forgive me again? I am sure she won't. Oh, no, she won't. And I deserve it, as usual! For I am wicked and make promises I never keep!" He came to the village late at night. It was so dark he could see nothing, and it was raining heavily. Pinocchio went straight to the Fairy's house, firmly resolved to knock at the door. When he reached it, however, he lost courage and ran back a few steps. A second time he came to the door and again he stepped back. A third time he repeated this performance. The fourth time, before he lost his courage, he grasped the knocker and made a faint sound with it.

He waited and waited. Finally, after a full half hour, a top-floor window (the house had four storeys) opened and Pinocchio saw a large Snail look out. A tiny light glowed on top of her head.

Who knocks at this late hour?" she called.

"Is the Fairy home?" asked the Puppet.

"The Fairy is asleep and does not wish to be disturbed. Who are you?"

"It is I."

"Who's I?"

"Pinocchio?"

"Who's Pinocchio?"

"The Puppet; the one who lives in the Fairy's house."

"Oh, I understand," said the Snail. "Wait for me there. I'll come down to open the door for you."

"Hurry, I beg of you, for I am dying of cold."

"My boy, I am a Snail and snails are never in a hurry." An hour passed, two hours, and the door was still closed. Pinocchio, who was trembling with fear and shivering from the cold rain on his back, knocked a second time, this time louder than before. At that second knock, a window on the third floor opened and the same Snail looked out.

"Dear little Snail," cried Pinocchio from the street. "I have been waiting two hours for you! And two hours on a dreadful night like this are as long as two years. Hurry please!"

"My boy," answered the Snail in a calm, peaceful voice, "my dear boy, I am a Snail and snails are never in a hurry." And the window closed. A few minutes later midnight struck; then one o'clock — two o'clock. And the door still remained closed! Then Pinocchio, losing all patience, grabbed the knocker with both hands, fully determined to awaken the whole house and street with it. As soon as he touched the knocker, however, it became an eel and wriggled away into the darkness.

"Really!" cried Pinocchio, blind with rage. "If the knocker is gone, I can still use my feet." He stepped back and gave the door a strong kick. He kicked so hard that his foot went straight through the door and his leg followed almost to the knee. No matter how he pulled and tugged, he could not pull it out. There he stayed as if nailed to the door.

Poor Pinocchio! The rest of the night he had to spend with one foot through the door. Finally, at dawn the door was opened. That kind snail had spent only nine hours coming down from the fourth storey to the door. She must have been in a great hurry!
"What are you doing there, with your foot through the door?" she asked, laughing.
"It was an accident. Won't you try, good snail, to free me from this trouble?"
"Well lad, this is a job for a carpenter, and I have never been a carpenter."
"Beg the Fairy to help me."
"The Fairy is sleeping, and mustn't be disturbed."
"But what can I do all day, with my foot stuck through this door?"
"You can amuse yourself counting the ants that are passing by."
"At least bring me something to eat, for I am terribly hungry."
"At once." said the Snail. And in fact, three and a half hours later Pinocchio saw her coming back with a silver tray on her head, holding some bread, a roast chicken and four ripe apricots. "The Fairy has sent you this breakfast." she said.

Seeing all those good things, the Puppet was quite relived. But how disappointed he grew when he discovered that the bread was plaster, the chicken made of board and the four apricots coloured plaster. He wanted to cry, and in his despair, he tried to throw away the tray and all that was on it; but instead, owing to his grief and his great weakness, he fainted.

When he came to himself, he was laying on a sofa and the fairy was beside him. "I shall forgive you once more," said the Fairy; "but never more if you misbehave again." Pinocchio vowed and promised that he would study, and always be good, and he kept his word for the rest of the year. He was first in the examinations and became the best scholar in the school. His conduct was so satisfactory and praiseworthy that the fairy was very pleased, and said:
"Tomorrow your dearest wish shall be granted."
"Do you mean .....?"
"Tomorrow you shall cease to be a wooden Puppet and become a real boy."

No one, unless they saw Pinocchio at that moment, could have any idea of his joy and gratitude. All his classmates were to be invited to the Fairy's house the next day to celebrate the important event. The Fairy prepared two hundred cups of coffee with cream, and four hundred bread rolls, buttered on both sides. The day promised to be a most happy one for all.

However, where Puppets are concerned, there is always a 'but' that can ruin everything.

XXX

PINOCCHIO, INSTEAD OF BECOMING A
BOY, RUNS AWAY TO THE LAND OF
JOY WITH HIS FRIEND LAMP-WICK.

Thrilled and delighted, Pinocchio asked the Fairy for permission to give out the invitations.

"Indeed you may invite your friends to tomorrow's party. Only remember to return home before dark. Do you understand?"

"I'll be back in one hour without fail," answered the Puppet.

"Take care, Pinocchio! Boys give promises very easily, but they as easily forget them."

"But I am not like those others. When I give my word I keep it."

"We shall see. In case you do disobey, you will be the one to suffer, not any one else."

"I know what it is to suffer for disobedience, I will do as you say." Without adding another word, the Puppet bid the good Fairy good-bye, and singing, he left the house.

In a little less than an hour, all his friends were invited. Some accepted quickly and gladly. Others had to be coaxed, but when they heard that the bread rolls were to be buttered on both sides, they all ended by accepting the invitation with the words: "We'll come if it makes you happy!"

Now, among his many friends Pinocchio had one whom he loved most of all. The boy's real name was Romeo, but everyone called him Lamp-Wick, for he was long and thin and had a woe-begone look about him. Lamp-Wick was the laziest boy in the school and the biggest mischief-maker, but Pinocchio loved him dearly. That day, he want straight to his friend's house to invite him to the party, but Lamp-Wick was not at home. He went a second time, and again a third, but still without success. Where could he be? Pinocchio searched here and there and finally discovered him hiding near a farmer's wagon.

"What are you doing there?" asked Pinocchio, running up to him.

"I am waiting for midnight to strike to go .... "

"Where?"

"Far, far away!"

"And I have gone to your house three times to look for you!"

"What did you want?"

"Haven't you heard the news? Don't you know what good luck is mine?"

"What is it?"

"Tomorrow I end my days as a Puppet and become a boy, like you and all my other friends."

"May you enjoy your good luck."

"Will I see you at my party tomorrow?"

"But I'm telling you that I go tonight."

"At what time?"

"At midnight."

"And where are you going."

"To a real country — the best in the world — a wonderful place!"

"What is it called?"

"It is called The Land of Joy. Why don't you come too?"

"I? Oh, no!"

"You are making a big mistake, Pinocchio. Believe me, if you don't come, you'll be sorry. Where can you find a place that will agree better with you and me? No schools, no teachers, no school books! In that blessed place there is no such thing as study. Here, it is only on

Saturdays that we have no school. In the Land of Joy, every day except Sunday, is a Saturday. Vacation begins on the first of January and ends on the last day of December. That is the place for me! All countries should be like that! How happy we should all be!"

"But how does one spend the day in The Land of Joy?"

"Days are spent in play and enjoyment from morn till night. At night one goes to bed, and next morning good times begin all over again. What do you think of it?"

"H'm ..!" said Pinocchio, nodding his wooden head, as if to say: " It's the kind of life which would suit me perfectly."

"Do you want to go with me, then? Yes or no? You must make up your mind."

"No, No, and again no! I have promised my kind Fairy to become a good boy, and I want to keep my word. Just see: The sun is setting and I must leave you and run. Good-bye and good luck to you!"

"Where are you going in such a hurry?"

"Home. My good Fairy wants me to return home before night."

"Wait two minutes more."

"It's too late!"

"Only two minutes."

"And if the Fairy scolds me?"

"Let her scold. After she gets tired, she will stop," said Lamp-Wick.

"Are you going alone or with others.?"

"Alone? No, there will be more than a hundred of us!"

"Will you walk?"

"At midnight the coach passes here that is to take us within the boundaries of that marvellous country."

"How I wish midnight would strike!"

"Why?"

"To see you all set out together."

"Stay here a while longer and you will see us!"

"No, no. I want to return home."

"Wait two more minutes."

"I have waited too long as it is. The Fairy will be worried."

"Poor Fairy! Is she afraid the bats will eat you up?"

"Listen, Lamp-Wick," said the Puppet, "are you really sure that there are no schools in The Land of Joy?"

"Not even the shadow of one."

"Not even one teacher?"

"Not one."

"And one does not have to study?"

"Never!"

"What a great Land!" said Pinocchio, with a feeling of longing. "What a beautiful Land! I have never been there, but I can well imagine it."

"Then why don't you come too?"

"It is useless for you to tempt me! I told you I promised my good Fairy to behave myself, and I am going to keep my word."

"Good-bye then, and remember me to the students at the grammar schools, at the high schools, and even at the colleges, if you meet them on the way."

"Good-bye, Lamp-Wick. Have a pleasant trip, enjoy yourself and remember your friends once in a while." With these words the Puppet started on his way home. Turning once more to his friend, he asked him:

"But are you sure that, in that country, each week is composed of six Saturdays and one Sunday?"

"Very sure!"

"And that vacation begins the first of January and ends on the thirty-first of December?"

"Very, very sure!"

"What a great country!" repeated Pinocchio, puzzled as to what to do. Then, in sudden determination, he said hurriedly:

"Good-bye for the last time, and good luck."

"Good-bye."

"How soon will you go?"

"Within two hours."

"What a pity! If it were only one hour, I might wait for you."

"And the Fairy?"

"By this time I'm late, and one hour more or less makes very little difference."

"Poor Pinocchio! And if the Fairy scolds you?"

"Oh, I'll let her scold. After she gets tired, she will stop." replied the foolish Puppet.

In the meantime, the night became darker and darker. All at once in the distance a small light flickered. A queer sound could be heard, soft as a little bell, and faint and muffled like the buzz of a far-away mosquito.

"There it is!" cried Lamp-Wick, jumping to his feet.

"What?" whispered Pinocchio.

"The coach which is coming to get me. For the last time, are you coming or not?"

"But is it really true that in that country boys never have to study?"

"Never, never, never."

"What a wonderful, beautiful, marvellous country! Oh-h-h!!"

XXXI

AFTER FIVE MONTHS OF PLAY, PINOCCHIO WAKES UP ONE FINE MORNING AND FINDS A GREAT SURPRISE AWAITING HIM.

Finally the coach arrived. It made no noise, for its wheels were bound with rags and straw. It was drawn by twelve pair of donkeys, all of the same size, but all of different colour. Some were grey, others white, and still others a mixture of brown and black. Here and there were a few with large yellow and blue stripes. The strangest thing of all was that those twenty-four donkeys, instead of being iron-shod like any other such animals, had on their feet laced shoes made of leather, just like the ones boys wear.

And the driver of the coach? Imagine to yourselves a little, fat man, much wider than he was long; round and shiny as a ball of butter, with a face beaming like an apple, a little mouth that always smiled, and a voice small and wheedling, like that of a cat begging for food. No sooner did any boy see him than he fell in love with him, and nothing satisfied that boy but to be allowed to ride in his coach to that lovely place called The Land of Joy. In fact the wagon was so closely packed with boys of all ages that it looked like a box of sardines. They were uncomfortable, they were piled one of top of the other, they could hardly breathe; yet not one word of complaint was heard. The thought that in a few hours they would reach a country where there were no schools, no books, no teachers, made these boys so happy that they felt neither hunger, thirst nor discomfort.

No sooner had the wagon stopped than the little fat man turned to Lamp-Wick. With bows and smiles, he asked in a wheedling tone:
"Tell me, my fine boy, do you also want to come to my wonderful country?"
"Indeed I do."
"But I warn you, my little dear, there's no room inside the coach. It is full."
"Never mind," answered Lamp-Wick. "If there's no room inside, I can sit on the top of the coach." And with one leap, he perched himself there.
"What about you, my love?" asked the little man, turning politely to Pinocchio.
"What are you going to do? Will you come with us, or do you stay here?"
"I stay here," answered Pinocchio. "I want to return home, as I prefer to study, and try to be useful in life."
"Much good may that bring you."
"Pinocchio!" Lamp-Wick called out. "Listen to me. Come with us and we'll always be happy."
"No, no, no!"
"Come with us and we'll always be happy," cried four other voices from the coach.
"Come with us and we'll always be happy," shouted the one hundred and more boys in the coach, all together."
And if I go with you, what will my good Fairy say?" asked the Puppet, who was beginning to waver and weaken in his good resolutions.
"Don't worry so much. Only think that we are going to a Land where we shall be allowed to make all the racket we like from morning till night."
Pinocchio did not answer, but sighed deeply once — twice — a third time. Finally, he said:
"Make room for me. I want to go, too!"
"The seats are all filled," answered the little man, "but to show how much I think of you, take my place as coachman."
"And you?"
"I'll walk."

"No, indeed, I could not permit such a thing. I much prefer riding one of these donkeys." cried Pinocchio. No sooner said than done. He approached the first donkey and tried to mount it, but the little animal turned suddenly and gave him such a terrible kick in the stomach that Pinocchio was thrown to the ground and fell with his legs in the air. All the boys laughed loudly, but the little man did not laugh, and walking quickly over to the kicking donkey, he pretended to pet and kiss it, but actually bit off half its right ear. Pinocchio was angry, and determined to get on its back, jumped high off the ground and this time, made a good landing, but this time the little beast kicked so high with his hind legs that the puppet was thrown onto a heap of stones by the side of the road. The boys, having applauded Pinocchio's leap onto the donkey's back, now shouted with laughter again. The small man went to the other side of the kicking animal, and bit off half of its left ear. "You can mount now, my boy." He then said to Pinocchio. "Have no fear. That donkey was upset about something, but I have spoken to him, and he should be quiet and reasonable now.

Pinocchio mounted and the coach started on its way. While the donkeys galloped along the stony road, the Puppet fancied he heard a very quiet voice whispering to him. "Poor silly! You have done as you wished, but you are going to be sorry before very long." Pinocchio, greatly frightened, looked about him to see whence the words had come, but he saw no-one. The donkeys galloped, the coach rolled on smoothly, the boys slept (Lamp-Wick snored like a dormouse) and the little, fat driver sang sleepily between his teeth:

"All night long they sleep,
But never any sleep have I ..."

After a mile or so, Pinocchio again heard the same faint voice whispering: "Remember, little Fool, boys who stop studying and turn away from school books and teachers just to give all their time to pleasure and foolish activities, sooner or later suffer greatly for it. Oh, how well I know this! How well I can prove it to you! A day will come soon when you will cry bitter tears, even as I am crying now — but then it will be too late!"

At these whispered words, the Puppet grew more and more frightened. He finally jumped to the ground, ran up to the donkey on whose back he had been riding, and taking its nose in his hands, looked into it's eyes. To his great surprise he saw that the animal was crying — crying just like a boy!
"Hey, Mr Driver!" cried the Puppet. "Do you know what a strange thing is happening — this donkey is actually crying, and large tears are running down his nose!"
"Let him cry. He may learn to laugh later!"
"Has he learned perhaps to speak!"
"No, he learned to mumble a few words when he lived for three years with a band of trained dogs."
"Poor beast"
"Come, come," said the little man, "do not let us lose time over a donkey that can cry. Mount quickly and let us go on. The night is cool and the road is long." Pinocchio obeyed without another word. The coach started again. Toward dawn the next morning they reached that much-longed for country, The Land of Joy.

This great Land was entirely different from any other place in the world. Its population, large though it was, was composed wholly of boys. the oldest were about fourteen years of age, the youngest, eight. In the street, there was such a racket, such shouting, such blowing of trumpets, that it was deafening. Everywhere groups of boys were gathered together. Some played at marbles, hopscotch, football, handball, others rode bicycles or sat

on merrygo-rounds. Here a group played circus, there another sang and recited, they walked on their hands, on stilts. Others dressed up as soldiers and drilled in companies. Laughter, shrieks, howls, cat calls, hand-clapping followed the parades. One boy made a noise like a hen, another, not to be outdone, crowed like a rooster, and another imitated a lion in his den. Altogether they created such a pandemonium that it would have been necessary for you to wear ear plugs if you were not part of the noisy crowd.

Immediately they got inside the city, Pinocchio, Lamp-Wick and the other boys who had come in the coach started out on a tour of investigation. They wandered everywhere, they looked into every nook and corner, house and theatre, and were delighted with what they found. There were squares filled with small wooden theatres, overflowing with boys day and night, both acting and as audience, and on the walls of the houses badly spelled words were written — Down with arithmetic! No more sums! No more School! Hurrah for The Land of Joy!

Pinocchio and Lamp-Wick made lots of friends. Who could be happier than they were, with lots of entertainment and parties. The hours, the days and weeks passed like lightning.
"Oh, what a beautiful life this is!" said Pinocchio each time that he met his friend.
"Was I right or wrong?" answered Lamp-Wick. "And to think you did not want to come! To think that even yesterday the idea came into your head to return home to see your Fairy and to start studying again! If today you are free from pens and books and school, you owe it to my advice, to my care. Do you admit it? Only true friends count, after all."
"Its true, Lamp-Wick, it's true. If today I am a really happy boy, it is all because of you. And to think that the teacher, when speaking of you, used to say, "Do not go around with that Lamp-Wick! He is a bad companion and some day he will lead you astray."
"Poor teacher!" answered the other, nodding his head. "Indeed I am of a generous nature, and I gladly forgive him."
"Great soul!" said Pinocchio, fondly embracing his friend.
Five months passed and the boys continued playing and enjoying themselves from morning till night, without ever seeing a school book, or a desk or a school. But, there came a morning when Pinocchio awoke and found a great surprise awaiting him, a surprise which made him feel very unhappy, as you shall see.

XXXII

PINOCCHIO'S EARS BECOME LIKE THOSE OF A DONKEY, IN A LITTLE WHILE HE CHANGES INTO A REAL DONKEY AND BEGINS TO BRAY.

Everyone, at one time or another, has found some surprise awaiting him. But there can be few of the kind which Pinocchio had on that eventful morning. On awakening, Pinocchio put his hand up to his head and there he found — Can you guess? He found that, during the night, his ears had grown at least ten full inches!

You must know that the Puppet, even from his beginnings, had very small ears, so small that to the naked eye they could hardly be seen. Think how he felt when he noticed that over night those two dainty organs had become as long as two floor brushes! He went

in search of a mirror, but not finding one, he just filled a basin with water and looked at himself. There he saw what he never could have wished to see. His head was adorned and enriched by a beautiful pair of donkey's ears.

It is not possible to describe the terrible grief, shame and despair of the poor Puppet. He began to cry, to scream, to knock his head against the wall, but the more he shrieked, the longer and the more hairy grew his ears. At those piercing shrieks, a Dormouse came into the room, a fat little Dormouse who lived upstairs. Seeing Pinocchio so grief-stricken, she asked him anxiously:

"What is the matter, dear little neighbour?"

"I am sick, my little Dormouse, very, very sick — and from an illness which frightens me! Do you understand how to feel the pulse?"

"A little."

"Feel mine then and tell me if I have a fever."

The Dormouse took Pinocchio's wrist between her paws and, after a few minutes, looked up at him sorrowfully and said:

"My friend, I am sorry, but I must give you some very sad news."

"What is it?"

"You have a very bad fever."

"But what fever is it?"

"The donkey fever."

"I don't know anything about that fever," answered the Puppet, beginning to understand all too well what was happening to him.

"I can tell you that, within two or three hours, you will no longer be a Puppet or a boy."

"What shall I be?"

"Within two or three hours you will become a real donkey, just like the ones that pull the carts to market."

"Oh, what have I done? What have I done?" cried Pinocchio, grasping his two long ears and pulling and tugging at them angrily, just as if they belonged to someone else.

"My dear boy," answered the Dormouse, trying to cheer him a little "why worry now? What is done cannot be undone, you know. It is well known that all lazy boys who hate books and schools and teachers, and spend all their days playing games or in idleness must sooner or later turn into donkeys." Tears are now useless. You should have thought of all this before."

"But the fault is not mine. Believe me, little Dormouse, the fault is all Lamp-Wick's."

"And who is this Lamp—Wick?"

"A classmate of mine. I wanted to return home, I wanted to be obedient, I wanted to study and to be successful in school, but Lamp-Wick said to me": 'Why do you want to waste your time studying? Why do you want to go to school? Come with me to The Land of Joy.

There we'll never study again. There we can enjoy ourselves and be happy from morning till night.'

"And why did you follow the advice of that foolish friend?"

"Why? Because, my dear little Dormouse, I am a heedless Puppet — heedless and heartless. If I had just a little more understanding I should never have abandoned that good Fairy, who loved me so well and who has been so kind to me! And by this time I should no longer be a Puppet. I should have become a real boy, like all these friends of mine! Oh, if I meet Lamp-Wick I am going to tell him what I think of him ... !"

After this long speech, Pinocchio walked to the door, but when he reached it, remembering his donkey ears, and feeling ashamed to show them in public, he turned back, and found a large cotton bag on a shelf, and put it on his head, pulling it far down to his very nose. Thus adorned he went out to look for Lamp-Wick. He was not to be found, and no-one had seen him. At last he found him where he lived.

"Who is it?" called Lamp-Wick when he knocked.

"It is I!" answered the Puppet.

"Wait a minute."

After a full half hour the door opened. Another surprise awaited Pinocchio! There in the room stood his friend, with a large cotton bag on his head, pulled far down to his very nose. At the sight of that bag, Pinocchio felt slightly happier, and thought to himself: "My friend must be suffering from the same sickness that I am! I wonder if he, too, has donkey fever?" But pretending he had seen nothing, he asked with a smile:

"How are you, my dear Lamp-Wick?"

"Very well. Like a mouse in a cheese."

"Is that really true?"

"Why should I lie to you?"

"Why then are you wearing that cotton bag over your head?"

"The doctor has ordered it because one of my knees hurts. And you, dear Puppet, why are you wearing that cotton bag down to your nose?"

"The doctor has ordered it because I bruised my foot."

"Oh, my poor Pinocchio!"

"Oh, my poor Lamp-Wick!"

An embarrassingly long silence followed these words, during which time the two friends looked at each other with a kind of mocking sympathy. Finally the Puppet, in a sweet voice said to his companion:

"Tell me, Lamp-Wick, have you ever suffered from earache?"

"Never. And you?"

"Never! Still, since this morning my ear has been torturing me."

"So has mine."

"Yours too?" And which ear is it?"

"Both of them. And yours?"

"Both of them, too. I wonder if it could be the same sickness."

"I am afraid it is."

"Will you do me a favour, Lamp-Wick?"

"Gladly!"

"Will you let me see your ears?"

"Why not? But before I show you mine, I want to see yours, dear Pinocchio."

"No, you must show yours first."

"Then let us make an agreement, let us take off our caps together. All right?"

"All right." Pinocchio began to count: "One! Two! Three!"

At the word "Three!" the two boys pulled off their caps and threw them high in the air. And then the Puppet and his friend, when they saw each other, both stricken by the same misfortune, instead of feeling sorrowful and ashamed, began to make fun of each other, and after much nonsense, they ended by bursting out into hearty laughter. They laughed till they cried.

But all of a sudden Lamp-Wick stopped laughing. He tottered and almost fell. Pale as a ghost, he turned to Pinocchio and said:

"Help, help, Pinocchio!"

"What is the matter?"

"Oh, help me! I can no longer stand up."

"I can't either," cried Pinocchio; and his laughter turned to tears as he stumbled about helplessly. They had hardly finished speaking when both of them fell on all fours and began running and jumping around the room. As they ran, their arms turned into legs, their faces lengthened, and their backs became covered with long grey hairs.

This was humiliation enough, but the most horrible moment was the one in which the two poor creatures felt tails appear. Overcome with shame and grief, they tried to cry and bemoan their fate. But what is done can't be undone! Instead of moans and cries, they burst forth into loud donkey brays, which sounded very much like: "Haw! Haw! Haw!"

At that moment a loud knocking was heard at the door and a voice called to them: "Open! I am the Coachman, driver of the coach which brought you here. Open I say, or I'll be very angry!"

XXXIII

PINOCCHIO, HAVING BECOME A DONKEY, IS BOUGHT BY THE OWNER OF A CIRCUS, WHO WANTS TO TEACH HIM TO DO TRICKS. THE DONKEY BECOMES LAME AND IS SOLD TO A MAN WHO WANTS TO USE HIS SKIN FOR A DRUMHEAD

Very sad and downcast were the two poor little fellows as they stood and looked at each other. Outside the room, the Little Man grew more and more impatient, and finally gave the door such a violent kick that it flew open. With his usual sweet smile on his lips, he looked at Pinocchio and Lamp-Wick and said: "Good work, boys! You have brayed well, so well that I recognised your voices immediately, and here I am." On hearing this the two donkeys bowed their heads in shame, dropped their ears and tucked their tails between their legs.

At first the Little Man petted and caressed them, and smoothed down their hairy coats. Then he took out a currycomb and worked over them till they shone like glass. Satisfied with the looks of the two little animals, he bridled them and took them to a market place far away from The Land of Joy, in the hope of selling them at a good price. In fact, he did not have to wait very long for an offer. Lamp-Wick was bought by a farmer whose donkey had died the day before. Pinocchio went to the Owner of a circus, who wanted to teach him to do tricks for his audiences.

And now do you understand what the Little Man's business was? He made a great deal of money by collecting foolish, disobedient boys, who hated school and discipline of any kind, and wanted to spend all their time playing, knowing that if they spent enough time just pleasing themselves they would become donkeys, and he could then sell them and make a good profit. So he drove around with his coach, and by flattery and promises carried the unworthy boys to The Land of Joy, so called, which offered all the games and play they desired, and then he just had to wait until they made little donkeys of themselves. He was a cruel, nasty little person.

And so Pinocchio and Lamp-Wick parted, and they never played together again. Pinocchio's new master took him, put him in a stable and filled his manger with straw, but after tasting a mouthful, spat it out. Then the man filled the manger with hay. But Pinocchio did not like that any better.
"Ah, you don't like hay either?" he cried angrily. "Wait, my pretty Donkey, I'll teach you not to be so particular." Without more ado, he took a whip and gave the Donkey a blow across the legs. Pinocchio screamed with pain and as he screamed he brayed:
"Haw! Haw! Haw! I can't digest straw!"
"Then eat the hay!" answered the master, who understood the Donkey dialect perfectly.
"Haw! Haw! Haw! Hay gives me a stomache ache!"
"I hope you don't expect me to give you chicken or cake." said the man, and, angrier than ever, he gave poor Pinocchio another lashing. At that second beating, Pinocchio became very quiet and said no more.

After that, the door of the stable was closed and he was left alone. It was many hours since he had eaten anything and he was becoming very hungry. Finally, not finding anything else in the manger, he tasted the hay, and chewed it well before swallowing it. "This hay is not so bad," he said to himself, "but how much happier I would be if I had stayed at home and became a real boy – I would be eating bread and jam and cake instead of hay!"

Next morning, when he awoke, Pinocchio looked for more hay, but he had eaten it all during the night. He tried the straw, but did not like the taste. "Patience" he said to himself. "If only those boys who do not wish to study, and leave home to get on that coach could know of these misfortunes, they would be saved this unhappiness. I must be patient.

Soon his master came to the stable. "Now my fine Donkey, I have not brought you here just to give you food and drink. Oh no! You are to help me earn a lot of money. I am going to teach you to jump and bow, to dance a waltz and a polka, and even to stand on your head."

Poor Pinocchio, whether he liked it or not, had to learn all these wonderful things, but it took him three long months and cost him many, many lashings before he was pronounced perfect. The day came at last when Pinocchio's master was able to announce an extraordinary performance. The announcements, posted all round the town and written in large letters, read:

GREAT SPECTACLE TO-NIGHT

LEAPS and **EXERCISES** by the **GREAT ARTISTS**
and **THE FAMOUS HORSES**
of the
C O M P A N Y

First Public Appearance
of the

FAMOUS DONKEY
P I N O C C H I O

Called

THE STAR OF THE DANCE

The Theatre was full an hour before the Show was scheduled to start. No seats were available anywhere in the house, at any price. The place was crowded with boys and girls, all in a fever of impatience to see the famous Donkey dance.

When the first part of the performance was over, the Ringmaster and Owner of the Circus, dressed up in a black coat, white knee breeches and shiny patent leather boots, introduced the donkey in a loud pompous voice, stating, among other things that Pinocchio was the 'most famous donkey in the world,' and had 'performed before the Kings, Queens and Emperors of all the great courts of Europe!' He continued by telling of his great difficulties in capturing and training the little animal, 'which had been grazing wild and free on the plains of Africa.' Every means of kind persuasion in training had failed, and he had finally been forced to use the whip to subdue the savage donkey, so that he had never been able to gain its affection, in fact it was still untamed, as could be seen by the fierce gleam in its eyes, However, he had found in the animal one great redeeming feature; due to a bump on its forehead, which had been proved by the Great Professor Gall to give a great talent for nimble footed movement, and rythmic dancing and jumping in animals, he had persevered, knowing that honoured audiences would greatly appreciate such a rare faculty. He therefore presented with pride this amazing animal and he hoped all the ladies and gentlemen present would truly enjoy its talents.

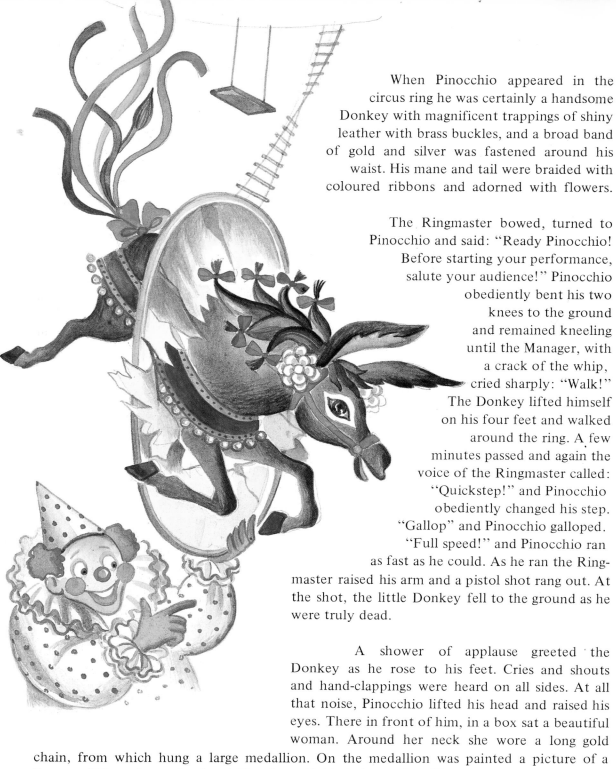

When Pinocchio appeared in the circus ring he was certainly a handsome Donkey with magnificent trappings of shiny leather with brass buckles, and a broad band of gold and silver was fastened around his waist. His mane and tail were braided with coloured ribbons and adorned with flowers.

The Ringmaster bowed, turned to Pinocchio and said: "Ready Pinocchio! Before starting your performance, salute your audience!" Pinocchio obediently bent his two knees to the ground and remained kneeling until the Manager, with a crack of the whip, cried sharply: "Walk!" The Donkey lifted himself on his four feet and walked around the ring. A few minutes passed and again the voice of the Ringmaster called: "Quickstep!" and Pinocchio obediently changed his step. "Gallop" and Pinocchio galloped. "Full speed!" and Pinocchio ran as fast as he could. As he ran the Ringmaster raised his arm and a pistol shot rang out. At the shot, the little Donkey fell to the ground as he were truly dead.

A shower of applause greeted the Donkey as he rose to his feet. Cries and shouts and hand-clappings were heard on all sides. At all that noise, Pinocchio lifted his head and raised his eyes. There in front of him, in a box sat a beautiful woman. Around her neck she wore a long gold chain, from which hung a large medallion. On the medallion was painted a picture of a Puppet. "That picture is of me! That beautiful lady is my Fairy!" said Pinocchio to himself. Recognizing her, he felt so happy that he tried his best to call out: "Oh my Fairy! My own Fairy!" but instead of words , a loud braying was heard in the theatre, so loud and so long that all the spectators — men, women and children, but especially the children — burst out laughing.

Then, in order to teach Pinocchio that it was not good manners to bray before an audience, the Ringmaster struck him on the nose with the handle of his whip. The poor little Donkey stuck out a long tongue and licked his nose for a long time in an effort to take away the pain. And what was his grief when on looking up toward the boxes, he saw that the Fairy had disappeared! He felt faint, his eyes filled with tears and he wept bitterly. No one knew it, however, least of all the Ringmaster, who, cracking his whip, cried out: "Bravo, Pinocchio! Now show us how gracefully you can jump through the rings." Pinocchio tried two or three times, but each time he came near the ring, he thought it easier to go under. In his unhappiness, he could not remember his training. The fourth time, at a look from his master, he leaped through, but one of his hind legs caught in the ring and he fell heavily to the floor. When he got up he was lame and could hardly limp as far as the stable.

"Pinocchio! We want Pinocchio! We want the little Donkey!" cried the children in the audience, but no one saw Pinocchio again that evening.

The next morning, the Veterinary Surgeon — that is, the animal doctor declared he would be lame for the rest of his life. "After all the time I wasted training him — what do I do with a lame donkey?" cried the Owner to the stable boy. "Take him to the market and get what you can for him."

When they reached the market square, a buyer was soon found.
"How much do you want for that little lame Donkey?" he asked.
"Four dollars"
"I'll give you four cents. Don't think I am buying him for work. I want only his skin. It looks very tough and I want to make myself a drumhead. I belong to a musical group in my village and need a drum." You can imagine how poor Pinocchio felt when he heard this conversation — he was to become a drumhead! A price was agreed on and the Donkey changed hands. His new owner took him to a cliff overlooking the sea, put a stone around his neck, tied a rope to one of his hind feet, and pushed him over into the water.

Pinocchio sank immediately, and his master sat on the cliff waiting for him to drown, so as to skin him and make a drumhead.

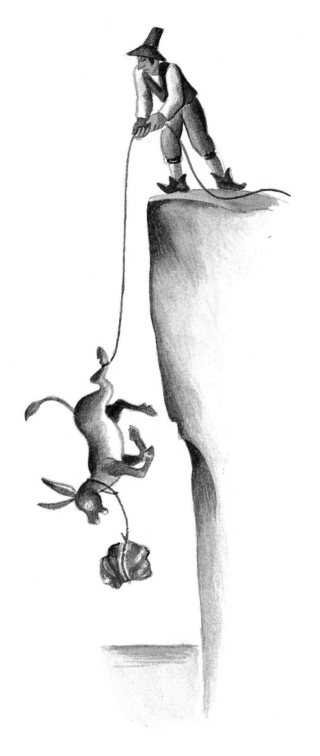

XXXIV

PINOCCHIO IS THROWN INTO THE SEA, EATEN BY FISHES, AND HE BECOMES A PUPPET ONCE MORE. AS HE SWIMS TO LAND, HE IS SWALLOWED BY THE TERRIBLE SHARK.

Down into the sea, deeper and deeper, sank Pinocchio, and finally, after fifty minutes of waiting, the man on the cliff said to himself: "By this time my poor little lame Donkey must be drowned. Up with him and then I can get to work on my beautiful drum." He pulled hard on the rope which he had tied to Pinocchio's leg — pulled and pulled and pulled, until at last he saw something appear on the surface of the water — but it was not the little Donkey — it was a very lively Puppet, wriggling and squirming like an eel.

Seeing the wooden Puppet the poor man thought he was dreaming, and sat there, his mouth wide open and his eyes popping out of his head. Gathering his wits together, he said:
"Where's the Donkey I threw into the sea?"
"I'm that Donkey," answered the Puppet, laughing.
"You? You're not a Donkey ... !"
"I was a Donkey."
"Ah, you little cheat — You're making fun of me."
"Not at all, dear Sir, I am quite serious."
"Well then, how is it that you, who a few minutes ago were a Donkey, now stand before me as a Puppet?"
"Perhaps it's the effect of the salt water."
"Don't you laugh at me, Puppet, or I will lose my temper, and you will go back into the sea, to join the Donkey."
"I will be happy to tell you my story, but first, will you kindly untie my leg?"
The man, who was unbelieving but curious to hear his tale, untied the rope knot and Pinocchio was free once more. He began his tale.

Well, once upon a time I was a wooden Puppet, just as I am today. One day I was about to become a boy, a real boy, but because I was lazy, hated books and lessons and had bad companions, I ran away from home. At first I had a good time, played with lots of friends and enjoyed myself, but one day I woke up to find myself changing into a Donkey with long ears, and even a tail! It was a shameful day for me! I hope you will never have one like it, dear Sir. Then I was taken to a fair and sold to a Circus Owner, who tried to make me dance and jump through rings. One night, during a performance, I had a bad fall and became lame. Not knowing what to do with a lame Donkey, the Circus Owner sent me to the market place and you bought me.
"I did indeed! I paid five cents for you. Now who will give me my money back?"
Well, after all, you bought me to do me harm, and drown me so that you could make a drum head!"
"I did! And now where shall I find another skin?"
"Never mind, dear Sir, the world is full of little donkeys!"
"Is this the end of your story, you little rogue?"
"Almost. I want to say that your thoughtfulness in putting a stone around my neck to shorten my suffering is appreciated, I shall always be grateful to you for that. But you see, you did not know of the love of my Fairy."
"What Fairy."

"She is my Mother, and she keeps an eye on me, however foolish I may be, and helps me when I get myself into trouble. For instance, when you threw me, as a little Donkey, into the sea to drown quickly, she sent a huge shoal of fish there to eat up the donkey body and release me — they did this in no time, one even kindly ate up my tail!"

The man gasped — "I shall never eat a fish again — imagine cooking a mullet and then finding a donkey tail inside it..!"

"I must say I agree with you, said the Puppet, laughing. "When eventually, the fish had finished eating my donkey coat, they found only my hardwood Puppet body, which they did not like, as they were afraid it would give them indigestion, so they turned and departed just as quickly as they had arrived, in a great shoal, and you pulled me up. That is my story and explains why you have pulled up a live Puppet instead of a dead Donkey.

"I think your story is nonsense" cried the man, angrily. I spent five cents to get you, and I want my money back, so I am going to take you to the market once more, and sell you as dry firewood."

"Very well, sell me if you can catch me" said Pinocchio, but as he spoke he gave a quick leap and dived into the sea. Swimming away as fast as he could, he called back "Good-bye Sir, if you ever need a skin for your drum, just call on me!"

After swimming for a long time, Pinocchio saw a large rock in the middle of the sea, a rock as white as marble. High on the rock stood a little goat bleating and calling and beckoning to the Puppet to come to her. There was something very strange about that little goat. Her coat was not white or black or brown as that of any other goat, but azure, a deep brilliant colour that reminded one of the hair of the lovely maiden. Pinocchio's heart beat faster. He redoubled his efforts and swam as hard as he could, toward the white rock. He was almost half way over, when suddenly a horrible sea monster stuck its head out of the water, an enormous head with a huge mouth, wide open, showing three rows of gleaming teeth, the mere sight of which would have filled you with fear. That monster was no other than the enormous Shark, which has often been mentioned in this story and which, on account of its cruelty had been nicknamed "The Attila of the Sea" by both fish and fishermen.

Poor Pinocchio! The sight of that monster frightened him almost to death! He tried to swim away from him, to change his path, to escape, but that immense mouth kept coming nearer and nearer. "Hurry, Pinocchio, I beg of you!" bleated the little goat on the rock. And Pinocchio swam faster and harder to reach her. "Faster, Pinocchio! The monster will get you! There he is! Quickly, or you are lost!" Pinocchio went through the water like a shot — swifter and swifter. He came close to the rock. The Goat leaned over and gave him one of her hoofs to help him up out of the water.

Alas, It was too late! The monster overtook him and the Puppet found himself in between the rows of gleaming white teeth. Only for a moment, however, for the Shark took a deep breath and, as he breathed, he drank in the Puppet as easily as he would have sucked an egg. Then he swallowed him so fast that Pinocchio, falling down into the body of the fish, lay stunned for half an hour.

When he recovered his senses, the Puppet could not remember where he was. Around him was a darkness so deep and black he could see nothing at all. He listened for a time and heard nothing. Sometimes a cold wind blew on his face. At first he could not understand where that wind was coming from, but later he understood that it came from the lungs of the monster. In fact this Shark suffered from asthma, so that whenever he breathed, a storm seemed to blow.

Pinocchio at first tried to be brave, but when he became convinced he was really and truly in the Shark's stomach, he burst into tears.
"Help! Help! he cried. "Oh won't some one come to save me?"
"Who is there to help you, my poor friend, said a rough voice, like a guitar out of tune.
"Who is that?" asked Pinocchio, frozen with terror.
"It is I, a poor Tunny swallowed by the Shark at the same time as you. And what kind of a fish are you?"
"I am a Puppet, not a fish."
"If you are not a fish, why did you let this monster swallow you?"
" I didn't let him. He chased me and swallowed me without enquiring who or what I was! And now what are we to do here in the dark?"
"Wait until the Shark has digested us both, I suppose."
"But I don't want to be digested," shouted Pinocchio, starting to cry.
"Neither do I," said the Tunny, but I am wise enough to think that if one is born a fish, it is more dignified to die under the water than in the frying pan."
"That may be so," cried Pinocchio, but I want to get out of this place – I want to escape."
"Well, go then, if you can."
"Is this Shark that has swallowed us very long?" asked the Puppet.
"His body, not counting the tail, is almost a mile long."
While talking in the darkness, Pinocchio thought he saw a faint light in the distance.

"What can that be?" he said to the Tunny.
"Some other wretched fish, waiting as patiently as we, to be digested by the Shark."
"I want to see him. He may be an old fish and know some way of escape."
"I wish you the best of luck, dear Puppet."
"Good-bye, Tunny. We may meet again."
"Who knows? It is better not to think about it."

XXXV

IN THE SHARK'S BODY
PINOCCHIO MAKES A
WONDERFUL
DISCOVERY

Pinocchio, when he had said good-bye to the Tunny, tottered away in the darkness toward the faint light, which glowed in the distance. As he walked; his feet splashed in a pool of greasy and slippery water which had a heavy smell of fish oil. The further he went the brighter and clearer grew the tiny light. When he finally reached it, he found — yes, it is quite unbelievable — he found a little table set for dinner and lighted by a candle stuck in a glass bottle; and near the table sat a little old man, white as snow, eating live fish. They wriggled so that, now and again, one of them slipped out of the old man's mouth and escaped into the darkness under the table.

At this sight the Puppet was filled with such great and sudden happiness that he nearly fainted. He wanted to laugh, to cry, to say a thousand and one things, but all he could do was to stand still, stuttering and stammering brokenly. At last, with a great effort, he was able to let out a cry of joy and, opening wide his arms he threw them around the old man's neck.

"Oh, Father, dear Father! I have found you at last? Now I shall never, never leave you again!"
"Can I trust my eyes, the old man said weakly, "I don't believe what I see — are you really my own dear Pinocchio?"
"Yes, yes! It is I! Look at me! And you have forgiven me, haven't you? My dear Father? I feel so ashamed that I caused you so much unhappiness — Oh, if you only knew how many things have happened, and how many troubles I've had since I left you ... And, enfolded in the old man's arms, he told his tale ... From the sale of the school book which had cost the old man his only overcoat, so he could enter the Puppet Theatre, meeting the

Fox and the Cat, and the Assassins, the good Fairy of the Azure Hair, his adventures in The Land of Joy, and he left out nothing. However, he related the stories without self-pity or bitterness, and acknowledged his own faults in the sometimes painful experiences.

Hearing of the flight on the pigeon and Pinocchio's attempts to reach the little boat, his Father said he had indeed recognised Pinocchio but he had been unable to turn the boat in the rough seas and had shortly afterwards been swallowed up by the Terrible Shark. "And how long have you been shut away in here?"
"Two long, weary years – which have been more like two centuries."
"And how have you lived? Where did you find the candle? And the matches with which to light it?"
"When the storm swamped my boat, a large ship suffered the same fate. The sailors were all saved, but the ship went down and the Shark swallowed most of it. The only thing he spat out was the mainmast, for it stuck in his teeth. Fortunately for me that ship was loaded with meat, preserved foods, crackers, bread, wine, cheese, coffee, sugar, wax candles and boxes of matches. With all these things I have been able to live on for two whole years, but now I am using up the last crumbs. There is nothing left in the cupboard, and the candle on the table is the last one. When it goes, we shall be in darkness.
"Then, my dear Father, said Pinocchio, "there is no time to lose. We must try to escape."
"Escape! How?"
"We can run out of the Shark's mouth and dive into the sea."
"Unfortunately, I cannot swim."
"Why should that matter. You can climb onto my shoulders and, as I am a fine swimmer, I can carry you to shore .
"That is a nice dream, my son, but do you think it possible for a Puppet a little over a metre high to have the strength to carry a man on his shoulders and swim so far?"
"We shall have to try it and see! If it is written that we must die, we shall at least go together, but there is no other way out."
Not adding another word, Pinocchio took the candle in his hand and, going ahead to light the way, he said to his Father: "Follow me, and have no fear."

They walked a long distance through the stomach and the whole body of the Shark. When they reached the throat of the monster, they stopped for a while to wait for the right moment in which to make their escape. The Shark, being very old and suffering from asthma and heart trouble, was obliged to sleep with his mouth open. Because of this, Pinocchio was able to catch a glimpse of the sky filled with stars as he looked up through the open jaws of his new – and he hoped, temporary, home.

"This is the right time to escape," he whispered to his Father. "The Shark is fast asleep. The sea is calm and the night bright as day. Follow closely, and we shall soon be saved." They climbed up the throat of the monster till they came to the immense open mouth. There they had to walk on tiptoes, for if they tickled the Shark's long tongue he might awaken – and where would they be then? The tongue was so wide and so long that it looked like a country road. The two fugitives were just about to dive into the sea when the Shark sneezed very suddenly and, as he sneezed he gave Pinocchio and Geppetto such a jolt that they found themselves thrown on their backs and dashed once more and very unceremoniously into the stomach of the monster. To make matters worse, the candle went out and Father and Son were left in the dark. "And now?" asked Pinocchio, looking very serious."
"Now we are lost."
"Never lost ... Give me your hand, Father, and be careful not to slip! We must try again."

With these words Pinocchio took his Father by the hand and always walking on, they climbed up the monster's throat for a second time. They then crossed the whole tongue and jumped over three rows of teeth. But before they took the last great leap, the Puppet said to his Father: "Climb on my back and hold on tightly to my neck. I'll take care of everything else." As soon as Geppetto was comfortably seated on his shoulders, Pinocchio, very sure of what he was doing, dived into the water and started to swim. The sea was like oil, the moon shone in splendour, and the Shark continued to sleep soundly.

XXXVI

PINOCCHIO FINALLY CEASES
TO BE A PUPPET AND BECOMES A BOY.

My dear Father, we are saved! cried the Puppet. "All we have to do now is to get to the shore, and that is easy." Without another word, he swam swiftly away in an effort to reach land as soon as possible. He suddenly noticed that Geppetto was trembling and shaking as if with a fever. Was this because he was frightened or cold? Perhaps a little of both, but Pinocchio, thinking his Father was frightened, tried to comfort him by saying:
"Have courage, Father! In a few minutes we shall be safe on land."
"But where is the shore?" asked the little old man, more and more worried as he tried to peer into the moonlit distance, "I can see nothing but sea and sky."
"I see the shoreline, " said the Puppet. Remember Father that I can see through darkness like a cat. I see better at night than by day."

Poor Pinocchio pretended to be unworried and optimistic, but in reality he was most unhappy about their position. Land was still far away and his strength was going, his breathing becoming more and more laboured. He felt he could not go on much longer. He swam on until he could no longer breathe, and then in despair cried out "Oh, Father, help, I am dying." Father and Son were really about to drown when they heard a voice, like a guitar out of tune, call from the sea: "Who is dying? What is the trouble?"
"It is I and my poor Father."
"I know the voice. You are Pinocchio."
"Yes indeed. And you?"
"I am the Tunny, your companion in the Shark's stomach."
"And how did you escape?"
"I followed your example. You showed me the way, when you left I followed."
"Tunny, you have arrived just at the right moment! I beg you to help us, or we are lost."
"With great pleasure. Just hang onto my tail, both of you, and I will take you to shore."

Geppetto and Pinocchio, as you can imagine, did not refuse the invitation. although, instead of of hanging on to the tail, they thought it better to climb on the Tunny's back.

"Are we too heavy?" asked Pinocchio.

"Heavy? Not at all, you are as light as seashells." answered the Tunny, who was as large as a horse.

As soon as they reached land, Pinocchio was the first to jump to the ground to help his old Father. Then he turned to the fish and said "Dear friend, you have saved my Father, and I have not enough words to thank you! Allow me to embrace you as a sign of my affection and eternal gratitude." The Tunny stuck his head out of the water and Pinocchio knelt on the sand and kissed him most lovingly on his cheek. At this warm greeting the Tunny, who was not used to such tenderness, wept. Then he felt so embarrassed that he turned quickly, plunged into the sea and disappeared.

In the meantime day had dawned. Pinocchio offered his arm to Geppetto, who was so weak he could hardly stand, and said: "Lean on my arm, Father and let us go. We shall walk very slowly, and if we feel tired we can rest by the wayside."

"Where are we going?" asked Geppetto.

"To look for a house or a hut, where they will be kind enough to give us something to eat, and some straw to sleep on."

They had not taken a hundred steps when they saw two rough-looking individuals sitting on a stone, begging. It was the Fox and the Cat, but one could hardly recognize them, they looked so miserable. The Cat, after pretending to be blind for so many years had really lost the sight of both eyes. And the Fox, old, thin and almost hairless, was tailless, for he had been forced to sell his beautiful tail to buy food.

"Oh, Pinocchio," he cried in a tearful voice. "Give some assistance to two poor old beggars, who are tired and sick."

"Sick!" repeated the Cat.

"Good-bye, false friends!" answered the Puppet. "You cheated me more than once, but you will never catch me again."

"Believe us! Today we are truly poor and starving."

"Starving!" repeated the Cat.

"You deserve to be poor! Remember the old proverb which says: 'Stolen money never bears fruit.' Good-bye."

"Do not abandon us."

"Abandon us" repeated the Cat.

"Good-bye, false friends. Remember another old proverb: 'Whoever steals his neighbour's shirt, usually, dies without his own.' "

After this meeting, Pinocchio and Geppetto went slowly on their way. Then they saw, at the end of a long road near a clump of trees, a tiny cottage, with a thatched straw roof.

"Someone must live in that little cottage," said Pinocchio. "Let us see for ourselves." They went and knocked at the door.

"Who is it?" said a little voice from within.

"A poor Father and a poorer Son, without food and with no roof to cover them." answered the Puppet.

"Turn the key and the door will open," said the same little voice.

Pinocchio turned the key and the door opened. As soon as they went in, they looked for the owner of the voice, but saw no-one.

"Where is the owner of the house?" cried Pinocchio, very much surprised.

"Here I am, up here!"

Father and Son looked up to the ceiling, and there on a beam sat the Talking Cricket.

"Oh, my dear Cricket," said Pinocchio, bowing politely.

"Oh, now you call me your dear Cricket, but do you remember when you threw a hammer at me to kill me?"

"I do, and I greatly regret it, because I understand better now what you were telling me. You are quite right, dear Cricket, and you can throw a hammer at me now, I deserve it! But please spare my poor old Father."

"I am going to spare both the Father and the Son. I just wanted to remind you of the trick you played on me long ago, to teach you that in this world of ours we must be kind and courteous to others if we want to find kindness and courtesy in our own days of trouble."

"I shall always remember the lesson you taught me. But will you tell me how you bought this little cottage?"

"This cottage was given to me yesterday by a little goat with azure blue hair."

"And where did the goat go?" asked Pinocchio.

"I don't know."

"And when will she come back?"

"She will never come back. Yesterday she want away bleating sadly and it seemed to me she said: 'Poor Pinocchio, I shall never see him again ... the Shark must have eaten him by this time.'"

"Were those her real words? Then it was she — it was — my dear Fairy," cried Pinocchio, sobbing bitterly. After he had cried a long time, he wiped his eyes and then he made a bed of straw for old Geppetto. He laid him on it and asked the Talking Cricket where he could get a glass of milk for his Father.

"Three fields away from here lives Farmer John. He has some cows. Go there and he will give you what you want."

Pinocchio ran all the way to Farmer John's house. The Farmer said to him: "How much milk do you want?"

"I want a full glass."

"A full glass costs a penny. First give me the penny."

"I have no money." answered Pinocchio, sad and ashamed.

"If you cannot pay me a penny I cannot give you any milk."

"That is too bad," said Pinocchio sadly, and started to go.

"Wait a moment," said Farmer John. "Perhaps we can come to terms. Do you know how to draw water from a well?"

"I can try."

"Then go to that well you see yonder and draw one hundred bucketsful of water."

"Very well."

"After you have finished, I shall give you a glass of warm sweet milk."

Farmer John took the Puppet to the well and showed him how to draw the water. Pinocchio set to work as well as he knew how, but long before he had pulled up the one hundred buckets, he was tired out and dripping with perspiration.

"Until today," said the Farmer, "my donkey has drawn the water for me, but now that poor animal is dying."

"Will you take me to see him" asked Pinocchio.

"Gladly."

As soon as Pinocchio went into the stable, he saw a little Donkey lying on a bed of straw in the corner of the stable. He was thin and worn out from hunger and too much work. After looking at him a long time, he said to himself: "I know that Donkey! I have seen him before." and, bending low over him, he asked, in donkey dialect: "Who are you?" At this question the Donkey opened weary, dying eyes and answered in the same tongue:

"I am Lamp-Wick." Then he closed his eyes and died.

"Oh, my poor Lamp-Wick," said Pinocchio in a faint voice, as he wiped his eyes.

91

"Do you feel so sorry for a little donkey that has cost you nothing?" said the Farmer. "I am the one who should be sorry – I paid good money for him."

"But you see, he was my friend."

"Your friend?"

"A classmate of mine."

"What," shouted the Farmer, bursting out laughing. "What! You had donkeys in your school? You must have studied hard!"

The Puppet, ashamed and hurt by these words, and saddened by the fate of his old friend, did not answer, but taking his glass of milk, he turned and walked home to his Father.

From that day on, for more than five months, Pinocchio got up every morning just as dawn was breaking and went to the farm to draw water. And every day he was given food and a glass of milk for his Father, who grew stronger and better every day. But he was not satisfied with this. He learned to make baskets of reeds and sold them. With the money he received, he and his Father were able to manage, living simply. Among other things, he built a wheel chair, strong and comfortable, to take his old Father out for an airing on bright, sunny days. In the evening the Puppet studied by lamplight. With some of the money he had bought himself a secondhand Reading book, and although a few pages were missing, he learned to read in a very short time. As far as writing was concerned, he used a long stick at one end of which he had whittled a long, fine point. Ink he had none, so he used the juice of backberries or cherries.

Little by little his diligence was rewarded. He succeeded, not only in his studies, but also in his work, and a day came when he put enough money together to keep his old Father comfortable and happy. Beside this, he was able to save the great amount of one hundred cents. With it he wanted to buy himself a new suit. One day he said to his Father: "I am going to the market place to buy myself a coat, a cap and a pair of shoes. When I come back I'll be so smartly dressed, you will not recognize me, and think you have a rich visitor!

He ran out of the house and up the road to the village, laughing and singing. Suddenly he heard his name called, and looking around to see where the voice came from, he noticed a large Snail crawling out of some bushes.

"Don't you recognize me?" said the Snail.

"Yes and no."

"Do you remember the Snail that lived with the Fairy with Azure Hair? Do you not remember how she opened the door for you one night and gave you something to eat?"

"I remember everything." cried Pinocchio. " Answer me quickly, pretty Snail, where have you left my Fairy? What is she doing? Has she forgiven me? Does she remember me? Is she very far away from here? May I see her?"

At all these questions tumbling out one after another, the Snail answered, calm as ever: "My dear Pinocchio, the Fairy is lying ill in a hospital."

"In a hospital?"

"Yes indeed. She has been stricken with trouble and illness, and she hasn't a cent left with which to buy a bite of bread."

"Really? Oh, how sorry I am! My poor, dear little Fairy! If I had a million I should run to her with it! But I have only one hundred cents. Here they are. I was just going to buy some clothes. Here, take them, little Snail, and give them to my good Fairy."

"What about the new clothes?"

"What does that matter? I should like to sell these rags I have on to help her more. Go, and hurry. Come back here within a couple of days and I hope to have more money for you!

Until today I have worked for my Father. Now I shall have to work for my Mother also. Good-bye, and I hope to see you soon."

The Snail, much against her usual habit, began to run like a lizard under a summer sun.

When Pinocchio returned home his Father asked him, "And where is the new suit?"

"I couldn't find one to fit me. I shall have to look again some other day."

That night, Pinocchio, instead of going to bed at ten o'clock, waited until midnight, and instead of making eight baskets, he made sixteen. After that he went to bed and fell asleep. As he slept, he dreamed of his Fairy, beautiful, smiling and happy, who kissed him and said to him: "Bravo Pinocchio! In reward for your kind heart, I forgive you for all your old mischief. Boys who love and take good care of their parents when they are old and sick deserve praise even though they may not be held up as models of obedience and good behaviour. Keep on doing so well, and you will be happy." At that very moment Pinocchio awoke and opened his eyes.

What was his surprise and his joy when, on looking himself over, he saw that he was no longer a Puppet, but that he had become a real live boy! He looked all about him and instead of the usual rough, poor surroundings he found himself in a beautifully furnished little room, the nicest he had ever seen. He jumped down from his bed to look on the chair standing near. There he found a new suit, hat, and shoes which fitted him perfectly. As soon as he was dressed, he put his hand into his pocket and found a little leather purse on which was written the following words:

The Fairy with Azure Hair
returns a hundred cents to her dear Pinocchio
with many thanks for his kind heart.

When he opened the purse he found fifty gold coins! Pinocchio ran to the mirror. He hardly recognized himself. Instead of the usual image of a cleverly made wooden Puppet, the bright and eager face of a tall boy looked out at him, with wide-awake eyes, and dark brown hair.

Surrounded by so much change and wonder, Pinocchio hardly knew what he was doing. He rubbed his eyes two or three times, wondering if he were still asleep or awake and decided that he must be awake.

"And where is Father?" he cried suddenly. He ran into the next room and there stood Geppetto, grown years younger overnight, spick and span in his new clothes. He was once again Master Geppetto, the wood carver, hard at work on a lovely wooden frame, decorating it with flowers, leaves and animals.

"Father, Father, what has happened? Tell me if you can," cried Pinocchio, as he ran and hugged him tight.

"This sudden change is all your doing, my dear Pinocchio," answered Geppetto.

"What have I to do with it?"

"Well, when bold, disobedient, unkind children become kind and good, they have the power to make their homes bright and new with happiness."

"I wonder what happened to the old, wooden Pinocchio?"

"There he is," replied Geppetto, pointing to a large Puppet leaning against a chair, head turned to one side, arms hanging limp, and legs twisted under him. After a long, long look, Pinocchio said to himself with great content: "How ridiculous I was as a Puppet! and how happy I am now that I have become a real boy!"